‘This is a skillful and deeply moving
piece of work.’
Guardian

‘A book to fall in love with.’
Julia Eccleshare, Lovereading4kids

‘Magical . . . This book is a delight.’
Katherine Rundell, author of *Rooftoppers*

‘Massively recommended.’
The Bookbag

‘I want to press it on every reading household.’
Awfully Big Blog Adventure

‘It is an irresistible read for a wide range of readers.’
Publishers Weekly

‘Outstanding 2015 Costa children’s winner asks
deep questions about courage and tyranny.’
Independent

‘The perfect gift.’
Telegraph

ABOUT THE AUTHOR

Kate Saunders is a full-time author and journalist and has written many books for adults and children. Her books for children have won awards and received rave reviews, and include Costa winner *Five Children on the Western Front*. Kate lives in London.

ALSO BY KATE SAUNDERS

Five Children on the Western Front
The Curse of the Chocolate Phoenix
The Whizz Pop Chocolate Shop
Magicalamity
Beswitched
The Belfry Witches
The Belfry Witches Fly Again
Cat and the Stinkwater War
The Little Secret

KATE SAUNDERS

FABER & FABER

First published in 2017
by Faber & Faber Limited
Bloomsbury House, 74–77 Great Russell Street
London, WC1B 3DA

Typeset in Plantin by M Rules
Printed in the UK by CPI Group (UK) Ltd, Croydon

A CIP record for this book is available from the British Library

ISBN 978–0–571–31084–5

For a boy,
a bear
and a penguin.

One

THE BOOK OF BLUEY

W HEN HOLLY DIED, Bluey suddenly fell silent and all the lights went out in Smockeroon.

Holly's bedroom was an empty cave that Emily was scared to walk past at night.

Men came to rip out the special lift for her chair, the huge hoist over the bath, and all the other things Holly didn't need any more.

Emily had grown up saying, 'My sister is disabled', and now she had to get used to saying, 'My sister is dead.'

It had happened nearly three months ago, at the beginning of the summer holidays. Holly had one of her seizures in the middle of the night, and this time, her heart stopped. Dad had used exactly those words when he told Emily – her heart stopped. When

1

nobody was looking, Emily put her hand on her own chest to feel the reassuring thud-thud-thud of her heartbeat. How did her heart know to keep on beating? It scared her to think what a fragile thing it was. People didn't realise how close they were to dropping dead. She overheard someone saying that her parents' hearts were 'broken' and worried that this would make them more likely to stop.

The counsellor at the hospital wanted Emily to talk about her feelings. She kept asking Emily about that morning, the terrible morning, when she woke to find Holly's room empty, and her parents sitting at the kitchen table like a pair of white-faced zombies. Everyone nagged you to 'talk', as if that solved everything.

'But I don't know how to say I miss Bluey,' she wrote in her secret book. 'I can't even say his name because it makes them cry.'

Bluey had been Holly's favourite toy – a bright blue teddy bear, always at Holly's side, for all the fifteen years of her life. He had a special place on her wheelchair, and on the metal frame of her bed. Long ago, as a very little girl, Emily had started doing a voice for Bluey. And then she had started telling stories about him, and the silly adventures he and Holly had when nobody was looking, in a magical land called Smockeroon. Emily had no idea where this word had come from, or how it had popped into her head, but it made Holly smile until her whole face lit up – though she couldn't talk and was nearly blind, she'd understood a lot more than people thought. Mum and Dad began to do Bluey's voice and repeat his daft sayings, until he lived with them like an invisible member of the family.

None of it had seemed real to Emily until Mum gave Bluey to the man from the undertakers, to put in Holly's coffin.

Emily couldn't find the words to explain why this made her so dreadfully sad. Of course Bluey had to be with his owner – that was the rule with toys. She didn't want her parents to think she cared more about a stuffed bear than she did about her sister. People who were in the first year of secondary school were supposed to be too old for soft toys, anyway. But Bluey had been so much more than a toy. Emily needed to remember as much about him as possible, because each memory of Bluey contained a bit of Holly.

This was why Emily had started the secret book –
to save Bluey. She had invented a fiendish code that
nobody (not even her best friend, Maze, who was
the queen of nosy parkers) would be able to read.
One of her birthday presents, a few months ago, had
been a small, chunky notebook with a bright pink
cover. Emily carried it everywhere. Whenever she
remembered something about Bluey or Smockeroon,
she wrote it carefully in her book, in tiny writing like
the tracks of an ant.

On the first day of her mother's new job, Emily
wrote: 'Toffee teapot.'

She was reminding herself about a story from
Smockeroon that had suddenly come back to her
during break – when Bluey had invited Holly to tea
and his new teapot had melted because it was made
of toffee.

Holly had liked the sound of words that began with
't'; she had smiled and made the huffing sound that
meant she was laughing.

Oh, Holly and Bluey, I miss you so much.

★

'It's just not fair,' said Maze. 'I shouldn't have to hang about at the surgery after school. It's so BORING – you won't let me use my phone and there's nobody to talk to.'

Maze (short for 'Maisie') Miller had been Emily's best friend since forever. Their gardens backed onto each other, so that they had always been able to run between the two houses without crossing any roads. She was a tall, confident person, with a loud voice, a big mouth and long black hair that she could sit on, and she was planning to be famous for something when she grew up. Emily was shorter and quieter, with thin blonde hair, a pale face and embarrassing big feet that she kept tripping over.

'Do stop moaning,' said Maze's mother. 'For the last time, I'm not leaving you alone in the house.' Maze's mum, Jo, was one of the doctors at the very busy local health centre, and this was her day to drive Maze and Emily home from their new school. 'You can always do your homework.'

'No I can't – I need some time to relax first. Don't blame me if I fail all my exams. You should've let me go to Summer's.'

Summer Watson was the most glamorous person in

their new class, and Maze was obsessed with her. She longed to be Summer's best friend and trailed after her like an adoring dog.

'What about Emily? According to the car rota, I'd still be picking her up – and then I'd have to drive across town again to fetch you, and I'm not your personal chauffeur.'

'Oh.' Maze glanced over her shoulder at Emily in the back seat.

The fact was that Maze had been weird since Holly died – distant, and not listening properly. When the two of them were alone she didn't want to talk, and even looked a little surprised when Emily spoke to her, as if she'd only just noticed she was there. This was painful, especially at school, where they were the only two girls from their primary school and didn't know anyone else. Sometimes Emily was so lonely that it was like being invisible.

'Let's hear from Emily, for a change,' Jo said, giving her a smile in the rear-view mirror. 'Today's your first time at Ruth's, isn't it? Well, I'm sure you'll be fine.'

'Oh, yes,' said Emily. 'Fine.' This wasn't true, but nobody wanted to listen to the truth, which was that she hated all the changes. They kept coming, one after the other, as if Holly's death had pulled the plug out of the whole world and sent it rushing down the drain.

First there was the stress of starting secondary school, where Emily had to meet strangers who didn't know about Holly and asked if she had brothers or sisters.

And as if that wasn't bad enough, Mum had got herself a part-time job with a local charity. On Thursdays and Fridays she would be working until six o'clock. And since Dad never got back before seven, she had arranged for Emily to go to the antique shop next door, which was owned by her friend Ruth.

'Your mum needs that job of hers,' Dad had told Emily firmly. 'She needs to get out of this house, where everything reminds her of—' He was bad at saying Holly's name, and gulped instead. 'And anyway, you like Ruth. You know you can trust her not to say anything silly about—' Gulp. 'People say silly things because they don't know what it's like and can't bear to imagine it. But she does know – she lost her son.'

Ruth's son had died when he was a teenager.

Young people weren't supposed to die. When you

had a dead young person in your family, it was like joining a weird club that nobody on earth wanted to be a member of.

Emily couldn't explain why she hated the new arrangement so much. It had nothing to do with Ruth. She wanted to go home – to run up the path and find Mum and Holly in the kitchen, waiting for the latest news from Smockeroon – and without Holly her home felt all wrong.

Jo stopped the car outside the shop, Barkstone Bygones. Emily got out, trying not to look at her empty house beside it.

'Catch you later,' Maze said. 'She won't let me text until I've done my homework.'

Barkstone had once been a village, and was now at the edge of the small market town of Bottleton, which was famous for only two things – a writer and a pie factory. The writer was John Staples, author of a series of classic sci-fi novels; until he died in the 1960s, he had lived in the red-brick house next door to Maze, and part of his long garden had been turned into a wildlife meadow. The pie factory was Norton's, a gigantic place beside the ring road, where Emily's dad worked in the accounts office. Emily and her parents lived in the old part of Barkstone village, in a small grey brick house beside a short row of shops. The shops were on the ground floor of a crazy old half-timbered building with a sagging thatched roof.

For a moment, Emily stood on the pavement, furiously blinking away a sudden rush of tears. The autumn day was grey, wet and gusty, and if Holly had been here, Bluey would have said something about the instant wellies he had invented (you sprinkled a sachet of magic powder on your legs and it turned into a pair of wellies, in a selection of tasteful colours). She had nearly forgotten. When she had a moment she would put it in the book.

Welly powder.

It only took a couple of words to pin a memory down.

Feeling more cheerful, Emily picked up her backpack and went into the shop. It was a very cosy place. The light came from two lamps with mouldy shades. There was a wood-burning stove and a sagging armchair covered with a splatter of faded roses. Ruth sold small pieces of furniture, china figures, dim silver jugs and speckled Victorian pictures. On the shelf behind her till, squashed between two big clocks, sat the most ancient of teddy bears, once the property of Ruth's mother. He was on the point of falling apart, but people had still wanted to buy him, so Ruth had hung a not-for-sale sign around his neck. On the wall above his head was a small photo of a handsome, laughing boy of ten or eleven – Ruth's dead son, Daniel.

'Hi, Emily,' Ruth said. 'Is it that time already? Don't worry, I hadn't forgotten you were coming and the kitchen's as warm as toast.' She was sitting beside the till, sorting through several boxes of the greetings cards she sold as a sideline. 'Your mum said I didn't have to feed you – but I couldn't miss such a great excuse for buying chocolate biscuits.'

Ruth was short and stout, with a springy puff of grey hair, and big round glasses with heavy frames. There was a china biscuit barrel at home in the shape of a smiling owl, and this had always reminded Emily of Ruth. Today she was particularly owlish, in a huge and shapeless brown cardigan; it really was amazing to see how neatly she dodged around the teetering heaps of stuff in her shop.

'Funny to see that blazer again – I was at Hatty Catty myself, back in the day.'

Emily's new school was called the Harriet Cattermole School for Girls; everyone in Bottleton knew it as 'Hatty Catty'. There was a uniform of dark purple blazer, white shirt, grey skirt and green-and-purple tie that still felt stiff and strange to Emily.

'I won't ask you if you're enjoying it,' Ruth said over her shoulder, waddling off towards the kitchen at the back of the shop. 'I hated my first term there – hated and loathed it. I was short and fat, and they called me "Spacehopper".'

'Wow – poor you!' Emily giggled, but only because it was so awful. 'What did you do?'

'Oh, it didn't last long; believe it or not, I ended up liking the place.'

'I don't exactly hate it,' Emily said, 'but I don't exactly like it, either. I suppose I'll just get used to it.' Her old school had been the small village primary round the corner. Hatty Catty was miles away, and enormous; there were huge crowds of big girls, clanging bells between lessons, and strict teachers who expected you just to know things by magic without being told. She couldn't imagine ever liking it.

'Well, give it a chance,' Ruth said. 'You never know.'

The kitchen was small and cluttered, dominated by a big old Rayburn that made it gorgeously stuffy and warm. Emily had often squeezed in here with her mother – and Holly, her wheelchair and her breathing machine – and found that she was feeling surprisingly relaxed and at home. Maybe this wouldn't be so bad, and it was only for two afternoons a week.

The table, just big enough for two people to sit at, was swamped by a very fat tabby cat, his striped belly hanging over a box of chocolate finger biscuits.

'Hi, Podge,' said Emily.

Ruth firmly shoved Podge down to the floor. 'You can do your homework here, and help yourself to the biscuits – I can't eat them because I've joined Weight Watchers again.'

'Thanks.'

'Anyway, I'll be in the shop till five – yell if you need anything.' Ruth waddled back to her chair beside the till and her boxes of cards.

Left alone with the lazy cat in the warm kitchen, Emily made herself a mug of tea and opened the biscuits. She did her homework (geography worksheet – not too bad). After that she took out her

Bluey book to write 'Welly powder'. The warmth was making her yawn.

And suddenly, before she even knew she had fallen asleep, she was dreaming.

In her dream she was telling a story to Holly, but she was also inside the story. A muffled, woolly, socky voice was singing something – Bluey's voice. The tune had been Dad's favourite for making up silly songs, the 'Toreador Song' from a famous opera called *Carmen*.

Bluey sang:

Help I have lost my lovely blue moustache!
I had it ON,
But now it's GONE!

And then his voice was joined by lots of other waffly voices – Bluey's choir. He had paid all Holly's other soft toys a penny a year to follow him round as a permanent backing group.

Oh WHERE is his lovely blue moustache?
Where oh WHERE has it GONE?

Emily opened her eyes to find that her head was resting on the table. She had been woken by a rumble of thunder; it was raining hard outside.

When had she ever made up a Bluey song about a moustache?

Two

THE WRONG DOOR

'Ruth, can I ask you something?'

'Hmm? Yes, of course.'

It was five o'clock. Ruth had shut the shop and joined Emily in the kitchen.

'After your son died, did you have dreams about him?'

Ruth wasn't embarrassed or distressed by this question. She looked thoughtful. 'I wanted to dream about him. But I didn't – not for a few years, anyway. Other people used to say they'd dreamt about him, and that made me jealous. Do you dream about Holly?'

'No,' Emily said. 'I go to sleep every night wishing I could dream about her, but I never remember anything in the morning.'

'That's probably because it happened so recently.'

Forgetting her diet, Ruth helped herself to three chocolate biscuits. 'Your mind is still in a state of shock. Danny only came back into my dreams when I stopped searching for him.'

'And were they . . . nice dreams?'

'Very nice,' Ruth said, with her mouth full. 'He was a happy little boy again, playing with his old friends in the enchanted forest.'

'What's the enchanted forest?'

'Oh, you know, the land of stories and imagination, where your toys go when you're not looking – funny and silly and kind, like Winnie-the-Pooh.' A big tear rolled down Ruth's cheek and splashed on the table. 'Danny called it the Land of Neverendings.'

'Sorry . . .' Emily was dismayed. She hadn't meant to make Ruth cry, and grown-up tears were horrifying.

'No, you mustn't say sorry.' Ruth tore off a piece of kitchen towel and blew her nose with a honking sound that made Podge twitch in his sleep. 'Look, I'll make a deal with you. We'll never get on if we're pussyfooting around each other's feelings. You let me cry about Danny and I won't make a big thing of it if you cry about Holly.'

'I cry every time I talk about her,' Emily heard

16

herself saying. 'And people think it's because I don't want to talk about her, so they change the subject. But I do want to.'

'Of course you do. And while you're here, you can talk about Holly as much as you like without worrying about my feelings. I'm not your parents.' Ruth scooped up the last chocolate biscuits. 'Deal?'

'OK,' Emily said.

It was a good idea. Talking to Ruth was not the same as talking to the counsellor, who had not known her sister and only thought of her as a disabled person. And Emily was interested in what Ruth had said about the enchanted forest, which sounded very like Smockeroon. Did everyone make up stories about the secret lives of their toys?

'I miss that glorious smile of hers,' Ruth said cheerfully. 'And I miss holding up Podge so she could stroke him.'

'Holly loved Podge,' Emily said. 'She loved it when we sat outside on hot days and he jumped into our garden – Dad said he was so fat he made a dent in the flowerbed.' There was a swelling inside her chest, and she didn't know if it would explode in laughter or tears.

Ruth blew her nose again. 'And, Lord, remember

that terrible cat fart he let off? I thought we were all being gassed!'

Just at that moment the fat cat hiccupped in his sleep, and Ruth and Emily burst out laughing. They couldn't stop laughing; they shrieked with laughter until Podge woke up and stomped off in an offended way that made them laugh harder.

Emily's mind went back to the day of the terrible cat fart. She'd made up a story for Holly, one of her best ones – how could she have forgotten? Podge had visited Smockeroon to be fitted with a fart warning system, a clever device that gave bystanders five minutes to clear the area before he let one off.

While Ruth – still giggling – made them more tea, Emily quickly pulled the pink notebook towards her and wrote: 'Fart Siren.'

Holly had loved the story; so had Dad, who was fond of comedy farting. When Holly was there, and they had something like beans for supper, he would make siren noises and say, 'Take cover, girls – it's the five-minute fart warning!'

He didn't do it nowadays.

There was another loud peal of thunder, followed by a flash of lightning.

'Ghastly weather!' Ruth came back to the table with their mugs of tea. Emily's mug was the one with the photo of Holly on it – her last Christmas present to Ruth. 'I hope you got some of the biscuits – I seem to have finished them.'

'Yes, thanks.'

They sat in silence for a moment.

Ruth said, 'Maybe I shouldn't tell you this – I've never told anyone. After my son died, I did have one dream. But it wasn't a good dream, and it wasn't about Danny.'

'You mean, it was a nightmare?' Emily's heart gave a little nervous jump.

'Well, yes. It was more of an atmosphere than anything else. A horrible atmosphere of sadness – and it came from Danny's bedroom. That's all, really.' Her voice was kind and she was looking at Emily very thoughtfully. 'When I woke up I dared to go into the room, and the sadness had gone. It was only empty – with a sort of loud, roaring emptiness that was the centre of all the emptiness in the house. But that was all.'

Emily knew about the emptiness; it was what made her afraid of Holly's bedroom. 'And . . . did the nightmare ever come back?'

'Oh, no. Never.'

'I had a nightmare when Holly died.' Emily hadn't told anyone about this, and it was hard to keep her voice from wobbling. 'I dreamt that she was calling to me. And when I went into her room, there was – well, it sounds silly, but I can't explain how horrible it was – there was a big black toad sitting in the middle of the bed. An evil toad.'

'You poor thing,' Ruth said softly. 'That doesn't sound at all silly to me.'

'I didn't tell Mum and Dad.'

'Don't worry, I won't either.'

'Thanks.'

'Pooh to my diet – let's open another packet of biscuits.' Ruth stood up. 'I've just remembered some custard creams.'

They ate biscuits, drank tea and watched *Love Your Garden* on the tiny, elderly television at one end of the dresser.

Telling Ruth about the black toad had been surprisingly easy. Maybe nightmares were normal when a person died, and didn't mean anything bad.

★

20

The worst of the storm came in the dead of night. Emily suddenly snapped awake when it was almost over and the bangs and crashes were already heading off towards the next town, like a very noisy circus parade. She sat up in bed and switched on her lamp. Her phone said it was a quarter to three in the morning. There was no sound outside except a deluge of rain falling, and a frog's chorus of gurgling gutters and drains.

She was just about to turn off the lamp and go back to sleep when she heard noises through the wall in Holly's bedroom.

For one confused second, before she remembered properly, she thought that Holly was ill – there had been so many emergencies in the middle of the night, when she had woken up to voices and footsteps, an ambulance flashing outside the window, and her mother saying everything was all right but she wouldn't be there in the morning.

But Holly was gone.

And these noises were different – soft thuds and scuttlings, that made Emily think of the time a squirrel had got into the ceiling above her parents' bedroom.

Mice? No, it was something bigger. Emily

shuddered. Perhaps a rat, or a fox. She was completely awake now, very nervous but prickling with curiosity.

I'll take a quick look, she decided, and if I can't chase the thing out, I'll wake Dad.

On the landing the noises were louder. The door to Holly's bedroom stood half open and she dared to look inside.

OK, so this is a dream.

She felt wide awake – but this had to be a dream. What she was seeing couldn't possibly be real.

A soft light glowed from the middle of Holly's empty bed. It came from a little tent – striped red and white, not more than knee-height, and with shadows moving about inside it.

Never in all her life would Emily forget the strangeness of what she saw next.

The tent flap opened and out strolled two rather battered soft toys – a short, round penguin, and a taller bear with bobbled light brown fur. The penguin was holding a newspaper, and the bear was carrying a picnic basket. Both toys were wearing false moustaches, fastened round their small, furry heads with elastic bands.

Emily watched, in a trance of astonishment, as the

bear opened the picnic basket, took out a tartan rug and spread it on Holly's bed.

And then the penguin spoke.

Actually *spoke*.

'What's going on? This isn't Pointed End!'

The bear said, 'It looks like a human bedroom. We must've come through the wrong door.'

'But there aren't any doors to the hard world in Deep Smockeroon! And we don't have a human bedroom any more. We're in a box in the attic.'

They came from Smockeroon, the land Emily had made up for her Bluey stories. But how could these toys know about Smockeroon, which only existed in her imagination, when she had never seen them before? Her heart was beating wildly; it was absolutely mesmerising to watch the soft yellow beak of the penguin opening and shutting as it talked. When she was little she had often wished her toys could come to life but the reality was decidedly creepy.

She moved closer to the bed. The toys took no notice of her.

'Well, this is a nice bedroom,' the bear said. 'Let's have our picnic, anyway.'

'Good idea, Smiffy,' said the penguin. 'I'm sure that human girl-person-thing won't mind.'

Emily said, 'I won't mind at all.'

The two toys gasped and stared up at her – the astonishment on their stitched-in faces was very strange to see, and looked so funny that Emily found herself smiling.

'Hugo!' whispered the bear. 'She can see us!'

'Yes, I can see you – and hear you. Who are you?' Emily bent down over the bed. 'Where did you come from?'

The toys quickly got over their surprise; their soft faces folded into friendly smiles, which looked even funnier.

'Hello,' the Penguin said. 'I'm Hugo and this is my best friend, Smiffy.'

'I'm Emily.'

She shook Smiffy's paw and Hugo's flipper; it was like shaking hands with two moving cushions.

'Is this your bedroom?' asked Smiffy.

'No. It used to belong to my sister Holly. And she died.' It was easy to say this to a smiling cushion.

'Oh, I see,' Hugo said, nodding wisely. 'That's why she's not here.'

'That would explain it,' said Smiffy. 'But it doesn't explain how we got here from Deep Smockeroon.'

Emily asked, 'What's Deep Smockeroon?'

'Oh, it's the nicest part,' said Hugo. 'It's for toys who live in Smockeroon all the time because their owners have left the hard world.'

'Hard world – does that mean real life?'

'Yes, we used to live in this world,' said Smiffy. 'We had a nice wide shelf in our owner's bedroom. But nowadays he comes to play with us in Smockeroon. It's much more convenient.'

'I see.' Emily was starting to feel dreamy and weightless, as if she was listening to a really fantastic story. 'Would you mind telling me why you're wearing those moustaches?'

Both toys looked surprised.

Smiffy said, 'It's the latest fashion in Pointed End – everybody's got a false moustache.'

'What's Pointed End?'

'That's our village in Smockeroon,' said Hugo. 'We built ourselves a lovely house there out of tinfoil and egg boxes.'

'But what if it rains – or maybe it doesn't rain there?'

'We get rain sometimes,' said Smiffy, 'but there's

always plenty of warning, so we have time to cover our house with a plastic bag. And it's held down with a brick to stop it blowing away.'

'Some people don't bother and just build themselves new houses,' the penguin said, puffing himself out importantly. 'Smiffy and I, however, are very proud of The Sycamores – I named our place The Sycamores to sound classy and posh, because we've decided to turn it into a boarding house for toys like us who don't have owners Hardside.' He held out the newspaper. 'You can read our advertisement.'

Emily wasn't scared now; talking to these strange toys felt comfortable and oddly familiar, as if she had slipped inside one of her own stories. She took the newspaper. It was small, about the size of a crisp packet, and printed in a mad mixture of different-sized letters. The big letters at the top of the newspaper said, THE STUFFED GAZETTE, and in slightly smaller letters, The InTeRestinG BiTs of the TrUth.

The headline on the front page said, DOoRBELL MONsteR STRiKes AgAln!

There was no time to read the story – Hugo reached out a flipper to turn the paper over to the back page, which was filled with advertisements.

REFinEd BOarding HouSe fOr IndePEndent Toys!
PriVIT jeLLy POnd!
DaNcinG and PArtiES!
LOTs of TeLEVisionS!
ThE SYCaMores
POintEd END
DEep SMoCKERooN.

Emily saw that the two strange toys looked proud, and kindly said, 'That's very good.'

'Thank you,' said Hugo. 'The "refined" part was my idea. We don't want any old riff-raff.'

Emily hardly heard him. She was staring, with a hammering pulse, at the advertisement underneath:

LOSt! ELEganT BLUe MouStachE!
PLeaSE return to BLUEY –
18 STIgGs COTTageS, PoinTEd EnD.

So it *was* Bluey's voice that she'd heard in her dream.

But Bluey had been burned inside Holly's coffin when she was cremated. All that remained of them both was a jar of ashes that Mum kept in her room.

'Don't cry!' Smiffy patted her hand with his soft brown paw. 'Why are you crying?'

'Sorry ... It's just that ... I'm sad because Bluey's gone.'

'But Bluey hasn't gone anywhere,' Hugo said. 'I saw him this morning.'

'What?'

'He waved to me from the other side of the jelly pond.'

'You mean ... Bluey's in Smockeroon?'

'Oh, yes,' said Smiffy. 'We often run into him. But he spends most of his time playing with his owner.'

'Holly! Oh, please – have you seen Holly?'

The world did a somersault. Emily was back in her bed, with no idea how she'd got there, crying with longing for her sister.

Three

CHOIR PRACTICE

'I DIDN'T WAKE UP UNTIL the fire engine came,' Maze said, 'but I saw the tree burning in the Staples's garden. The flames were YAY high before they could put it out and the guy next door was really scared that his shed would catch – the sparks were flying everywhere.'

They were in the classroom before the first lesson, and Maze was describing the drama of last night's storm to Summer Watson and her cool friends. Emily had missed the amazing sight of the old oak tree in flames; this morning she had opened her bedroom curtains to the shocking spectacle of its blackened branches rising from a sea of mud.

'And the tree looks completely weird now,' Maze went on. 'All charred and sort of leaning over.'

'Scary,' said Summer, tossing back her long blonde hair (Maze had started to imitate the hair tossing). 'I've never seen anything that's been struck by lightning.'

Emily was invisible again, but it meant she had more time for her report. She was writing all the details of last night's mad experience in the Bluey book and it was taking ages – the lines of tiny writing made her hand hurt.

The bear and the penguin saw Bluey.
Bluey is still alive in Smockeroon.
He lives in Pointed End and plays with the owner he never stopped loving.

Maze ignored her all day. Summer was in the car with them on the way home. She was having tea at Maze's house. Emily was not going. She had not been invited. It was embarrassing to sit there feeling like a big unwanted lump. Maze showed off intensely. There was a lot of hair tossing.

It was a relief to get into the dusty warmth and quiet of the antique shop.

'Hi, Emily!' Ruth suddenly bounced up from

behind the armchair. 'I'm just putting down some mouse pellets – I'm sure I heard mice in the loft last night, and it's no use expecting Podge to do anything about it.' She was wearing the owlish brown cardigan again, and did not seem to have noticed that one sleeve was grey with dust. 'I went up there with a torch and didn't see anything – but the little beasts are good at hiding.'

So Ruth had also heard weird noises last night. This was interesting enough to take Emily's mind off Maze and Summer Watson.

'Were you woken up by the storm?'

'Don't tell me you managed to sleep through it – I've never heard such a racket!' Ruth put the 'Please ring' sign in the window and briskly shut up the shop. 'Nobody's going to be buying antiques on such a dismal afternoon – let's go into the kitchen.'

The weather was dark and windy, with cold spatters of rain that hit the windows like fistfuls of gravel. Ruth's kitchen was warm, messy and welcoming and there was a large treacle tart in the middle of the table. Emily sat down, relaxing for the first time that day. Podge ambled over to lie down on her feet.

Ruth made tea and asked polite questions about Mum's new job. Once she had cut them both handsome slices of the treacle tart, however, she was back on the subject of the storm.

'I think I must've been having some sort of dream – I woke up because I had to write something down – something of huge, global importance. That's when I heard the noises in the loft, and a second later we were in the thick of a raging thunderstorm. I came downstairs to make a cup of tea, and I actually saw the Staples tree being struck by lightning!'

'I was shocked when I saw it this morning,' Emily said, wincing over the super-sweetness of the treacle tart. 'I suppose they'll have to cut it down now.'

'That might be a problem, because it's a slightly famous tree and the Staples fans will make a fuss. There's an old photo of Staples and his brother and sister sitting under that tree as children. The local paper's doing a story about it.' Ruth brushed pastry crumbs off her dress and cut herself another large slice of tart. 'Do you like his novels?'

'Yes, and so does my Dad. And I love the films.'

Ruth chuckled. 'My son said the Staples books were

"boring" and "nothing but elves making speeches", and when I tried to read one to him, he hurled it out of the window.'

Emily wanted to hear more about Ruth's dream. 'What was it that you had to write down?'

'Oh Lord, it's so silly!' Ruth snorted with laughter. 'When I finally went back to bed I saw that momentous message, and it was just two words – "label glue".'

'Label glue – does that mean anything?'

'It's from the stories I used to tell Danny when he was little. "Label" was a rude word to his toys, the equivalent of "bum". You know how some soft toys have labels stitched to them, with washing instructions and so on?'

'Yes!' Bluey's label had said 'Wipe with a damp cloth'.

'I'd completely forgotten,' said Ruth. 'I can't imagine what jogged it out of my memory.'

'Maybe it was because we were talking about dreams yesterday,' Emily suggested.

'Yes – or it could've been something to do with the storm, and the electricity in the atmosphere.'

Emily wondered if the electricity had caused her mad vision last night. She couldn't shake off a feeling that something else had happened during the storm; something much bigger.

★

In her dream that night there was singing – a happy, rather tuneless chorus of sweet, woolly, socky voices, singing what sounded like the Christmas carol 'I Saw Three Ships', but with different words.

> *I saw an egg box sailing by*
> *With my FRIEND in Pointed END,*
> *And it was filled with cake and PIE,*
> *In Pointed End in the MORNING!*

Emily woke up very slowly, with a feeling that something soft was moving on top of the duvet around her feet. She half opened her eyes, and her heart gave a jump of joy. The strange toys had come back, just as she'd hoped. The funny little red-and-white tent, glowing with soft, mysterious light, stood on the rug beside her bed.

There were more of them now. Emily counted seven small shapes. Hugo, the bossy penguin, was

34

conducting a choir. Smiffy the bear was here, with another three stuffed bears. And – weirdest sight of all – there were two Barbie dolls, in the long black robes and veils of old-fashioned nuns. Had there ever been such a thing as a nun Barbie?

'Well, that wasn't bad,' said Hugo. 'Not bad at all – especially now we're all singing the same song. But we've got a lot of work to do if we want to win the September Sing-Song Prize.'

One of the Barbie nuns gave a scornful sniff. 'I thought there'd be more of us! Where's Mr Sale? Where's that grand German lodger of yours?'

'I told you – Notty Sale is still working Hardside,' said Hugo. 'And our German lodger has done nothing but sleep since he arrived, which means he needs to rest from his secret job. They'll come when they can.'

Emily watched them dreamily, her eyes half-open, fascinated.

'I certainly hope so,' the nun said coldly. 'Come, Sister Toop, the tea horn will be going any minute.'

She stood up and walked across Emily's foot; her hard plastic feet tickled and Emily let out a yelp of laughter.

'Good gracious!' squeaked the nun. 'The human! Would somebody please tell me what she's doing here?'

Properly awake now, Emily sat up in bed – carefully, so she didn't disturb the toys – and switched on the bedside lamp. The group of toys looked even funnier and odder in the lamplight. None of them were wearing false moustaches this time.

'Hello, Emily,' said Smiffy. 'We just popped in for choir practice.'

'There's something funny about that door,' Hugo said, shaking his head. 'It's the same old door in the wall at the bottom of our garden and it normally comes out by the shops. We didn't mean to come to a human's bedroom.'

'It's a different bedroom this time,' said Smiffy.

'I don't like humans,' said the Barbie nun.

'But you're a toy,' Emily pointed out. 'Isn't it your job to like humans?'

'Sister Pretty had a bad experience,' said Smiffy. 'That's why she became a nun. You see, the nun costume covers up her scars.'

'Scars?' It was startling to hear this harsh word coming from a soft toy.

Sister Pretty drew herself up proudly. 'You might not believe it now, but I was once a beautiful doll with long golden hair. Unfortunately, my human

36

owner was a selfish, careless girl. In the hard world I live at the bottom of a mouldy cardboard box in the loft.'

'So – is that where you are now?' Emily was getting confused. 'What I mean is, if I found that box right this minute, would you be in it?'

'Well, of course!' Sister Pretty rolled her eyes, as if Emily had asked a very silly question. 'Dear me, doesn't this human know anything about toys? We can always be summoned back to the hard world, where we really are. When no humans are watching, however, we can go where we like. At least' – she frowned – 'we can go back to Smockeroon. I don't know how we managed to get into the hard-world bedroom of a total stranger. Please don't take it personally, but my ghastly little owner put me off your kind for life!'

'Poor you,' said Emily politely, feeling a twinge of guilt about a Barbie that had belonged to her when she was small; she hadn't a clue where it was now.

'It hurts all the more,' Sister Pretty went on, 'because she was the one who started me off. She played with me and made up stories about me. Her imagination sparked me into being. But then she forgot about me, and didn't even care when her horrible big brother attacked me!'

'What did he do?'

Sister Pretty whispered, 'I can't talk about it!'

'It was dreadful!' The other Barbie nun spoke for the first time – she was a very beautiful black Barbie, and her lovely face was perfectly clean. 'He scribbled on her!'

All the toys looked so serious that Emily tried not to laugh.

'I decided to become a nun,' said Sister Pretty, 'because the veil covers the hideous scars on my face.'

She took off her nun's veil, to reveal the word 'bum' written on her forehead in blue biro.

'Oh, how awful!' Emily said, as kindly as she could. 'Let me wash it off for you—'

'That's kind of you, dear. But my scars can only be washed off in the hard world.'

'I don't have any scars,' the other nun said happily. 'I'm a limited-edition black Barbie in a purple ballgown, and in the hard world I'm still in my plastic box. Somebody collected me, and he imagined a life for me, even though he wouldn't open my box. I decided to be a nun to keep Pretty company.'

Sister Pretty scowled. 'This is Sister Toop,' she told Emily coldly. 'Short for "Too pretty".'

'Pretty gets a bit jealous sometimes,' Smiffy said.

The three smaller bears were huddled together at the end of the bed, whispering and giggling. Now that she looked at them properly, Emily saw that they were pretty little pastel-coloured girl-bears – one pink, one pale blue, one yellow – and they were wearing smart red hats, with the letters 'S-R' in blue sequins.

'Have we finished choir practice?' the yellow bear asked. 'Because I'm getting a bit bored.'

'Hush, Pippa!' said Sister Pretty. 'Stop being difficult!'

'I'm not being difficult,' said Pippa. 'We've got to get back to the factory.'

'Er – sorry?' Here was another unexpected word; Emily did not remember any factories in her stories about Smockeroon.

Hugo tugged at her sleeve with his soft black flipper. 'They're all Seam-Rite Girls,' he said importantly, as if he expected Emily to be impressed. 'That means they work in the Seam-Rite factory. It's the leading brand of seam cream.'

'But toys don't have jobs,' Emily protested. 'Toys don't have to work!'

This made all the toys chuckle.

'Of course we don't have to work,' said Pippa. 'We go to the factory because it's so much fun!'

The only factory Emily knew was Norton's, where Dad worked; though he liked his job and the other people in his office, it wasn't exactly what you'd call 'fun'. Lately he'd been under a lot of stress with the paperwork for some sausage rolls.

'We sing a bit, and we dance a bit,' said the pink Seam-Rite Girl. 'And we pose for photos. We're sort of celebrities in Smockeroon because we do the adverts on television.'

The three bears began to sing:

Seams BRIGHT!
Seams TIGHT!
Got to get the seams RIGHT.

'They're chosen because they're beautiful,' Sister Pretty said bitterly. 'Nobody scribbled on them.'

'I'm certainly beautiful enough to be a Seam-Rite Girl!' Sister Toop whipped off her nun's veil to reveal a mass of glorious black hair. 'But I don't have seams!'

'Hahahaha!' giggled all the Seam-Rite Girls.

'BAG!' screamed Sister Pretty. 'QUICK BEFORE I FAINT!'

With a sigh, Sister Toop pulled a brown paper bag from her pocket. 'Do I have to?'

'QUICK!'

'OK, keep your hair on.' The beautiful black Barbie pulled the bag over her head, totally covering her face.

'Sometimes I get so jealous of her that it makes me faint,' Sister Pretty explained to Emily. 'That's why I thought of the bag. I need a few minutes to get over it.'

Emily couldn't help laughing at this; luckily the toys did not seem to be offended. 'Isn't that a bit mean? It's not her fault!'

A new voice suddenly called from the floor. 'Oh, here you all are – I've been looking everywhere!'

'Hi Notty,' said Hugo.

A toy came out of the striped tent and when she saw him, Emily gasped aloud. It was a very, very old bear, sagging and baggy and held together with pieces of sticking plaster. He had no ears, which made his

41

bald head look very strange. He was pulling a little shopping trolley. Around his neck hung a sign: 'Not For Sale.'

It was the bear who sat behind the till at Ruth's shop.

What on earth was he doing in her bedroom?

This dream . . . wasn't a dream.

'You must've gone through the wrong door.' Notty's voice was muffled and mouldy-sounding. 'Have I missed choir practice?'

'No,' said Hugo, 'but we'd better have it somewhere else because this bedroom belongs to this human called Emily.'

'What?'

'I said, we're in the wrong place.'

'Eh?'

'He can't hear,' said Sister Pretty. 'He's taken his ears off again – I keep telling him.' She hurried to the edge of Emily's bed and shouted, 'MR SALE, PUT YOUR EARS ON!'

'What?'

All the toys shouted together, 'EARS!'

'Why are you all whispering? Hang on – I'll get my ears.' The ancient toy rummaged in his shopping trolley until he pulled out a pair of furry ears and stuck them back on his bald old head. 'Now, what were you saying?'

'We did NOT come through the wrong door,' the penguin said sternly. 'I think we ended up in the hard world because the door is BROKEN. I'd better report it to the Sturvey.' Though he wasn't wearing any clothes, Hugo somehow appeared to take something out of his pocket – a mobile phone, which looked odd until Emily remembered inventing a toys' phone for Bluey.

'What's the Sturvey?'

All the toys chuckled, as if Emily had asked a really silly question. There were mutterings of 'She's never heard of the Sturvey!' and 'Can you believe it?'

'The Sturvey is in charge of things,' said Hugo.

'I mean, is it a person? Or is it like the government?'

'It's where all of the imagination comes from,' said Smiffy. 'If there's a problem, the Sturvey always fixes it.'

'So is it a sort of power station?'

'I don't have time to explain now.' Hugo was punching numbers on his phone. 'I've got to make my report.'

'But . . . make your report to WHAT?' asked Emily.

'Do shut up, dear,' said Sister Pretty. 'Hugo, put it on speaker.'

The penguin pressed a button and the room was filled with the sound of an old-fashioned phone ringing.

This was incredible – a sound from Smockeroon.

A dusty voice said, 'You have reached the central office of the Sturvey. If your house has blown away, press One. If you've forgotten your name and address, press Two. If you're applying for a playground extension, press Three. If it's anything else, please leave a message after the beep.' After a short pause, the voice added, 'Beep!'

Hugo said: 'I wish to report a broken door between Deep Smockeroon and Hardside. It's at the bottom of the garden at The Sycamores, Pointed End. Thank you.'

'That should do it,' said Sister Pretty. 'Now let's go back to Deep Smockeroon to finish our choir practice.'

'Quite right,' said Notty. 'Some of our friends can't come Hardside because they don't exist here any more. Bluey was quite cross.'

'Bluey! You've seen Bluey!' Emily cried out. 'You spoke to him!'

44

'Hello, Emily.' The frayed stitches of the bear's mouth lifted into a friendly smile. 'Yes, I saw him just now.'

Emily's eyes prickled with tears of longing; suddenly she could see Bluey in her mind's eye incredibly clearly, in his old place on Holly's bed. And Holly's face when she was happy and not ill. And the fact that she wasn't here hurt as much as ever.

She asked, 'Could you give him a message?'

'Of course,' said Notty.

'Tell him ...' There were so many things she wanted to say.

I hate it without you and Holly.

I wish I could come to Smockeroon.

Please tell Holly how much I miss her.

'Just tell him Emily says hi and sends her love.'

'OK,' said Notty. 'Come along, everybody.'

'Wait a minute,' Emily said. 'Please don't go yet! I still don't understand about the Sturvey. And where are your false moustaches?'

'Oh, moustaches are so over!' sniffed Sister Pretty.

'The new fashion is all about hats,' Hugo explained. 'But we couldn't bring them here because they're made of cake.'

'Cake hats? Seriously? Does Bluey have one?'

'Of course – today he was looking very smart in a Black Forest Gateau, with special holes cut for his ears.'

'Please wait!' Emily had been about to start crying but was distracted by the sight of the toys jumping off her duvet and vanishing into the little tent on the floor. The penguin was the last through the flap. He gave her a cheery wave with his flipper, and the striped tent popped like a soap bubble and disappeared.

Four

BLACK TOAD

WEEKENDS WERE VERY QUIET these days.
When Holly was alive, Mum and Dad had
made a big thing of going out as much as possible,
and finding new places where they could take
Holly, her wheelchair and her breathing machine.
Now that she was dead they could go anywhere –
but they didn't want to. They sat around at home,
hardly saying a word, as if waiting for something,
and watching each other warily for signs of sadness.
For some reason they were all pretending not to
be sad.

On the Saturday morning after her vision (she
refused to call it a 'dream') of the toys' choir practice,
Emily passed the time writing her report in the
Bluey book. She would usually have run through the

back gardens to Maze's house, but Maze was over at Summer's, on the other side of Bottleton, and she didn't want to see anyone else.

Dad said, 'We should be celebrating the new job – let's have lunch at the Royal Oak.'

This had been a regular treat when Holly was alive.

'Yes,' Mum said slowly, looking at Emily. 'It's time we did that again. I don't want Neil and Mandy to think we don't like them any more.'

Neil and Mandy, the owners of the local pub, had always been very kind to Holly. They kept a special table for the family, with room for the wheelchair and an electric socket for the breathing machine. There was a framed picture above the bar of Holly, smiling radiantly, with Neil and Mandy on either side of her dressed up as chickens; it had been taken two years ago, at a charity fun run.

This was the first time they had been to the Royal Oak without Holly. The special table was no longer there; as Mandy explained, it was never a very good table, stuck between the toilets and the fruit machine. Without Holly, they could sit at a far nicer table in the conservatory. Neil brought them all free drinks. The three of them sat in near silence, looking through rain-pebbled glass at the dreary pub garden.

I wonder if my voice still works.

I should have died too.

It can't be much worse than this.

The world looks the same but everything has turned sad.

Emily had started writing things in her Bluey book that had nothing to do with Smockeroon – all the things she couldn't say aloud because people got upset, or agitated, or embarrassed.

In the garden, on the other side of the glass, there were small stone ornaments in the shapes of animals – a hedgehog, a rabbit, a cat. But there was something new today, and when she saw it, Emily turned cold.

Why did they buy that evil-looking black toad?

Her mother said, 'This is easier than I thought. I was afraid that . . . but it's actually nice to be in a place where she was happy.'

'I've missed this steak and kidney pie,' said Dad. 'What are you staring at, Em?'

'The new statue.'

'The what?'

When Emily looked again, there was no statue of a toad; just a coil of black hosepipe, distorted by the rainy window.

She turned back to her parents, 'Nothing.'

★

At school on Monday morning, before the first lesson, everyone was talking about the end of term play, *Alice in Wonderland* – especially Maze and Summer, who expected to have starring roles.

'It's a bit babyish,' Maze said, 'but at least we'll be up on that huge stage, with proper lighting. And I know you'll be playing Alice. I mean, you've got the blonde hair, just like Alice in the book – and you're so talented.'

Summer had done a lot of acting, most famously in a television advert for B&Q. Acting was now Maze's latest mania. They were both planning to be major international stars by at least Year Ten.

'I was hoping for a proper musical,' Summer said. 'Like *Grease* or *Wicked*.'

'Oh yes, your singing is so wonderful . . .'

Emily was glad when the lesson started. Their

English teacher, Ms Robinson, was younger and less scary than the other teachers at Hatty Catty. She was black, pretty (for a teacher) and wore cool clothes (for a teacher). Emily mainly liked Ms Robinson because she didn't notice when she wrote in her Bluey book during lessons.

The chunky notebook was filling up. In the beginning she had only jotted down a couple of words at a time, just enough to jog her memory. Now she had to report every mad detail of what she had seen.

I know Holly has gone.
But is part of her alive in Smockeroon?
Did Bluey pass on my message?
Who, or what, is the Sturvey?

Ms Robinson began to talk about the play. She called Summer and Maze to the front of the class to read a short scene between Alice and the Caterpillar. They acted brilliantly and loudly, and Emily felt free to tune out.

Could I talk to Holly through the toys?
'Emily.'
Does Holly miss me?

'Emily Harding!'

She raised her head from the Bluey book, and the whole class was staring at her. Heat flooded into her cheeks.

Ms Robinson said, 'I asked you to read the part of Alice.'

Emily's attention snapped back to the real world. Ms Robinson was holding out a piece of paper. Feeling very clumsy and awkward and wishing she could disappear, Emily shut the notebook and went to the front of the class.

'And Martha, you can be the White Rabbit.'

Emily breathed more easily. She'd been dreading having to act with someone like Summer, but Martha Bishop was nice – plump and sweet-faced and friendly. And she was so good as the White Rabbit that Emily forgot about being awkward and having huge feet and started to pay proper attention to the story. It was a story she knew very well; Dad had read the book to her when she was little, and she had loved the Disney cartoon. But she had not seen the connection until now.

Alice fell down the rabbit hole and came out in Wonderland.

What if there's a rabbit hole that could get me to Smockeroon?

When the bell rang for the next lesson, it took Emily a few minutes to put her Bluey book safely inside the hidden pocket of her backpack, and she was the last girl left in the classroom.

Ms Robinson shut the door. She walked across to Emily and sat down at the next desk. She was very serious, and for one nervous moment Emily thought she was about to get a telling-off. But her teacher wasn't angry.

'You were very good just now, Emily.'

'Thanks.'

'It's the first time I've seen the real you. Most of the time, you're not really here, are you? You're always scribbling away in your notebook or staring out of the window.'

Emily didn't know what she was meant to say to this; it was embarrassing that the teacher had noticed.

Ms Robinson said, 'When I was nine, my little brother died.'

'Oh.' This was unexpected, and jolted Emily into looking at her teacher properly for the first time.

'I'm telling you because I want you to know that I know how it feels – OK? If you ever need to get away from everything, you can come to me and I'll square it with the other teachers.'

'I'm all right,' Emily said.

'His name was Lenny.' Ms Robinson's voice softened and her face was suddenly much younger. 'He was seven and he was my partner in crime. When he died I didn't know what to do with myself.' She took her phone from her pocket, scrolled through her photos, and held up a picture of a grinning little boy with his front teeth missing. He was wearing a red demon costume with plastic horns. 'That's him at Hallowe'en.'

'What did he die of?'

'Meningitis. It happened so quickly – I was in shock for months.'

Emily wondered if she was 'in shock'; could that be the reason she was seeing all these weird things? 'He looks . . . nice.'

'I still miss him every day,' Ms Robinson said. 'That pink notebook of yours – are you writing about your sister?'

'Yes – sort of.'

'I used to write secret letters to Lenny – just bits of news. "Dear Lenny, today we went to Nan's", or "today we went swimming". I couldn't stand him being left out of things.'

Emily said, 'He looks like you.'

'Thanks – now you have to show me a picture of Holly.'

Nobody ever asked to see a picture of Holly. Emily took her phone out of her backpack and showed Ms Robinson her favourite – Holly sitting in the sun outside the back door, with Bluey perched on top of her head.

'She's lovely,' Ms Robinson said. 'And her eyes are just the same as yours – anyone can see that you're sisters.'

'And our hands were the same – the same shape I mean.'

'You'll always be sisters. Nothing and nobody can ever take that away.' Ms Robinson stood up, brisk and teacher-like again. 'Any time you want to talk about her, you can come to me – just remember that.'

'Thanks,' Emily said.

She felt a little less of a freak for the rest of the day, and she didn't have a chance to write anything more in her Bluey book because Martha Bishop decided to sit next to her at lunch. It was nice to have someone to sit with, and Martha's cheerful stream of chatter was very entertaining.

It helped to know that Ms Robinson understood about living without Holly because her little brother had died. But she couldn't possibly understand everything else.

★

Barkstone Bygones had been closed for a couple of days. This was not unusual; Ruth often went off hunting for antiques at jumble sales and country auctions. When it was still closed on Thursday, however, Emily was worried; could Ruth have forgotten that this was one of the days she was coming after school?

She bent down and called through the letterbox. 'Ruth – are you there? Ruth! It's Emily!'

A dim light snapped on at the back of the shop. 'Coming!'

A few minutes later, Ruth opened the door. Her owl-shaped body was wrapped in a red tartan

56

dressing gown and she looked awful – baggy-eyed, with a grey tint to her skin.

'You're ill,' Emily said. 'You should've told us.'

'I'm not ill,' Ruth said. 'Not according to the doctor, anyway. He says I don't have a brain tumour and I haven't had a stroke. It's all stress, apparently.'

'Oh.' Emily was uneasy; this sounded like good news, but Ruth didn't seem to think so. 'Can I do anything – maybe go round to the shop for you? If you don't want me here, I could go to Mum's office . . .'

'No,' Ruth said, rubbing her forehead wearily, 'I do want you here. In fact, I think you may be the only person I can talk to.'

'Me? What do you mean?'

'You might think I'm completely bonkers, but I can take it from you.' With a sudden burst of energy she pulled Emily into the darkened shop and locked the door. 'Come into the kitchen, and try not to notice the mess.'

Emily followed her through the obstacle course of knick-knacks in a high state of curiosity; whatever Ruth was about to tell her, this was the most interesting conversation she'd had for ages.

On her way past the till, she glanced up at the shelf, and there was the ancient bear in his usual place, with his not-for-sale sign hanging round his neck. In her mind she said, Hi Notty – but he looked like a toy again, with his dim glass eyes and stitched-on smile, and it was impossible to imagine him as anything else.

Maybe I was dreaming after all.

'I've been living on toast and marmalade for the past few days,' Ruth said. 'Just brush off the crumbs.'

Emily sat down in the least crumby chair. The small table was crowded with empty jars, sticky plates and mugs half filled with cold tea. Everything was covered with crumbs, even Podge, sitting in a lazy heap of fur on the floor.

Ruth hastily dumped most of the dirty crockery into the sink. 'Look, I'd be really grateful if you don't tell your parents about all this.'

'OK.'

'Let me make some more tea – I'm still trying to work out how to explain it.' She made two mugs of tea and plumped down into the other chair opposite Emily. 'Do you know what "hallucination" means?'

Emily's mouth was dry. 'When you see something that isn't there.'

58

'Exactly – something that isn't there, though it feels perfectly real when it's happening. It definitely wasn't a dream.'

'You saw something?'

'I'll start at the beginning,' Ruth said, with a frown of concentration. 'I was watching TV in my little sitting room upstairs. I nodded off for a few minutes, and when I woke up, I suddenly had one of those moments . . .' She halted, searching for the right words. 'My son died nearly ten years ago, but sometimes it hurts as if it happened yesterday. I expect you know how that feels.'

Emily nodded, knowing exactly.

'Well, this is where the hallucinations begin, so let me be perfectly clear, I was not asleep. And yet I had the strangest feeling that something dreadful had got in downstairs – something that soaked the whole house in darkness and despair. There was a noise, too – like a great crowd of gnats whining – but as I went downstairs and got closer, I realised that it was the noise of hundreds of people crying and sobbing. And then I saw it, on the floor beside the cat flap – a huge black toad.'

'What?' Emily gasped. 'My evil toad?'

'Yes! It was a horrible, shiny black blob, with such an awful expression in its eyes – but this is the really bonkers part.' Ruth took a deep breath. 'The next thing was that I heard a voice. And it wasn't a human voice.'

'What was it?' Emily hardly dared to breathe.

'It sounded sort of fuzzy,' Ruth said. 'I turned round and nearly keeled over with amazement – it was my mother's old bear! He was running across the kitchen floor and he was singing a song – something like: "Shoo! Shoo! You smelly old Pooh!"'

Neither of them smiled at this.

'He had a little can of aerosol and he sprayed the toad with a cloud of pink glitter,' Ruth went on. 'It gave a sort of angry croak, and then it disappeared into a crack in the floor, like a hideous, oozing blob of black oil.'

They were quiet for a moment, listening to the wind outside.

'That's when I decided I must've had a stroke, or some kind of brainstorm. Even though the doctor swore I was fine.'

Emily shivered.

I'm not the only one.

'If you've had a stroke,' she said carefully. 'Then . . . so have I.'

Slowly, she began to tell Ruth about the little tent she had seen on Holly's bed and the strange toys. She was concentrating so hard on the story that it took her a minute to notice Ruth's reaction.

Her face had frozen into a look of terrified amazement. And when Emily got to the part about the names of the penguin and the bobbled bear being Hugo and Smiffy, she started to cry.

'Ruth?' She reached across the table to touch Ruth's arm. 'Did I say something wrong? I promise I'm not making this up.'

'Wait there!' Ruth gave a loud sniff and bounced up out of her chair. 'Don't move!'

She rushed upstairs. Emily heard doors opening and distant thumps, and Ruth falling off something and swearing. Ten minutes later she was back in the kitchen, covered with dust and clutching a large cardboard box. It had 'DANIEL' written on the side in black marker. Emily helped to clear a space on the table and Ruth put the box down.

'There were some things he loved so much that I could never throw them away, because I loved them too.' She opened the box and took out two faded, squashed soft toys – a bear and a penguin.

And Emily cried out, 'But that's them – that's Hugo and Smiffy!'

Five

WONDERLAND

EMILY AND RUTH GAPED at each other in astonishment, horror, fascination. The silence between them stretched out, until Emily was afraid she'd said something wrong.

'Good grief!' Ruth whispered.

'I'm not making it up,' Emily said again, rather fiercely. If Ruth didn't believe her, she would sink through a crack in the floor like the black toad. 'They moved and they talked. I know what I saw.'

Ruth stroked the soft toys. 'Hugo and Smiffy!' She wasn't crying now, but looked dazed. 'I've told so many stories about these two! When Danny was little I had to make up a new adventure for them every night – and you met them!'

'I told you, they just appeared in my bedroom.'

'Right, let's start again.' Ruth was suddenly businesslike and vigorous. 'Your mother will be back soon, and I want to hear all the details. Wait a sec – I need some very strong coffee, and there's not a decent biscuit in the house! Run round to Pauline's and get us a big packet of something chocolatey.'

Pauline was the lady who ran the small supermarket at the end of the row of shops. While Ruth made coffee, Emily hurried out to buy the biscuits, so intensely alive with excitement that her every sense was tingling. Though she was only gone for a few minutes, the whole atmosphere of the shop was different by the time she got back.

Ruth had swapped the tartan dressing gown for one of her embroidered sacks. She had swept up most of the crumbs and brushed the cobwebs from her springy grey hair. Her blackened coffee pot hissed and bubbled on the hot plate. The cardboard box was now on the floor and Hugo and Smiffy sat on the table, leaning against the wall.

'Ah, classic milk-chocolate digestives – perfect! I know your mother doesn't approve, but please help yourself to one of my evil sugary drinks.'

'Thanks.' Emily was only supposed to have Coke at

weekends, and this was Thursday. But it was a special occasion; as special as it got.

Finally, they sat down with their drinks and Ruth opened the biscuits.

'You've met my son's old toys and I've met your black toad.' She stuffed a biscuit into her mouth. 'There it is, and neither of us is crazy. I did wonder if we both had some weird illness – in medieval times, there was something called ergot poisoning, which was caused by mouldy wheat and made whole villages as mad as March hares. But I looked it up on the internet, and if we had ergot poisoning we would have hacked each other to pieces by now. Let's assume we're both in our right minds – take me back to the beginning. Don't leave anything out.'

Ruth was a good listener. Her brown eyes were huge and serious behind her thick round glasses.

Emily began with the Bluey song she'd heard in her dream – she even sang it. The words poured out of her. Ruth nodded, sometimes raising her eyebrows, occasionally throwing in a comment.

'Smiffy's false moustache was orange, wasn't it?'

'Yes – how did you know?'

'It was his favourite colour. Once, when Danny

and I were on holiday in Devon, I knitted Smiffy a little orange scarf.' Ruth bent down, rummaged in the cardboard box and pulled out a grubby, toy-sized scarf. 'Danny was six, and he liked it so much that I had to knit another one for Hugo – a purple one – oh, this is so weird! Please go on, and don't mind me.'

The relief of letting it all out made Emily as light as a feather.

Ruth chuckled over the Barbie nuns, saying she'd never heard of such a thing. 'But I do know about Seam-Rite, the leading brand of seam cream. I made it up when one of Hugo's seams burst and I had to mend it.'

'And what about the Sturvey – did you make that up too?'

'No, this is the first I've heard of anything called the Sturvey. Is it a person – I mean, a stuffed person – or a thing?'

'I don't know,' said Emily. 'But the toys seem to think the Sturvey can fix the broken door between Smockeroon and our world. When you told your stories to Daniel, who was in charge?'

'Nobody. Nothing. The Land of Neverendings didn't have any sort of ruler.'

'So how did the Sturvey get into my imagination?' Emily asked. 'And how did the toad get into your imagination?'

'That,' said Ruth, 'is the great question. Why would our imaginations join up? And why now? I mean – how is it possible that we were telling stories about the same place? But do go on – you say Hugo and Smiffy have opened a boarding house for toys?'

'Yes, for toys who don't have owners Hardside. Hugo called it The Sycamores because he thought it sounded posh.'

'Hmm, typical Hugo,' Ruth said, smiling but very thoughtful. 'He always was rather a snobbish penguin. His hobby was making important speeches.'

'I can believe that.' Emily reached for another biscuit and crammed it into her mouth. 'He likes bossing people about, doesn't he?'

'Lord, yes – Danny decided Hugo was the President of the Penguin Society. They had a wonderful HQ in the middle of town, with a snow machine and a swimming pool.' Ruth knocked back the last of her coffee. 'But the massed penguins were so noisy that they got chucked out, and they had to move to the remote countryside – and Hugo always

67

got huffy if you mentioned it. "For your information, Daniel, we were not chucked out, we were asked to leave, which is quite different!"' She stopped, and her smile faded. 'Sorry, I didn't mean to gabble at you. How extraordinary that it's all hanging about in my memory, after all these years!'

A silence settled around them. The really important part of the story was looming, and neither wanted to be the first to mention it.

'The toys saw Bluey, Holly's bear,' Emily said. 'I couldn't see him. He got cremated and doesn't exist any more. But in Deep Smockeroon he has a cottage and a hat made of cake. And he still goes off to play with his human owner – and so do Hugo and Smiffy.' A knot of pain swelled in her chest, and for a couple of seconds the longing for her sister was so intense that she couldn't speak. 'If I could get to Smockeroon I could see Holly – I can picture it in my head so clearly. I think she'd still have her chair, which was part of her, and in my Bluey stories it was a magic flying chair.'

'But she wouldn't need that wretched breathing machine,' Ruth said. 'Not in any enchanted forest worthy of the name. And she wouldn't need all those

68

tubes sticking out of her. Horrid things like pain and sadness simply do not exist in that forest.' She let out a long, long sigh. 'How unbearably lovely, to think of my Danny popping back there to visit his old mates! He never completely grew out of it all – even when he was a towering sixth-former, years after I stopped telling the stories, he used to write the date of the annual Penguin Society outing in the calendar.'

They were both crying and neither of them cared. Ruth tore off two sheets of kitchen roll so they could mop up the tears that slid down their cheeks.

Emily's tears ran in straight lines. Ruth's tears took a more winding route along her grooves and wrinkles. She blew her nose in a series of loud honks – why did old people blow their noses so loudly?

Suddenly, everything felt calm and back to normal.

Emily said, 'Please don't say anything about this to my parents, or they'll make me have therapy.'

'Don't you worry, I won't breathe a word to anyone – I don't want people to think I've lost my marbles.' Ruth helped herself to yet another biscuit. 'Did you make up the word "Smockeroon"?'

'Yes.' Emily was sure about this.

'I have the strangest sense that I've heard it before

somewhere, that's all. I wish I knew where. That's going to bother me for days.'

A sharp knock on the door made them jump. Emily's mother was back from work and neither of them had noticed the time.

Mum said, 'Didn't you hear me? I was knocking round the front for ages!'

'Sorry, we got carried away,' Ruth said. 'We were talking about ... er ...'

'My history homework,' Emily said quickly. 'Ruth was helping me.' She raised her eyebrows meaningfully. 'See you tomorrow.'

Her mother wasn't exactly suspicious, but she looked at Emily rather oddly when they got home.

'I'm glad you're getting on so well with Ruth.'

'She's nice,' Emily said.

'Oh, I know she's nice,' Mum said. 'But I didn't expect to find the two of you gossiping like that – like you and Maze. Come to think of it, we haven't seen Maze for ages – why don't you ask her round on Saturday?'

'Maybe.' Emily hadn't told her parents that Maze was no longer her best friend. 'I'll see how I feel.'

★

'I think there's a very simple reason why people love the story of *Alice in Wonderland*,' Ms Robinson said. 'It's about discovering a secret, magical world – and who hasn't dreamed of doing that? Hands up everyone who checked the back of the wardrobe when they first read about Narnia!' She raised her own hand, and there was a scatter of giggling. 'When I was little, I made up a game called "Tableland". My mother had to put a big cloth over the kitchen table, and then I'd crawl underneath and pretend that I'd slipped into another dimension – just like Alice falling down the rabbit hole.'

It was the last lesson of the week, double English. And this afternoon they were in the assembly hall, where all the chairs had been cleared away to leave a vast expanse of empty floor. Emily had not been able to tune out, or to write in her Bluey book. This was the first official rehearsal for the end of term play, and Ms Robinson had kept them busy – she made them do the silly Caucus Race, in which everybody wins, and it had been so totally hilarious that they were all sitting or lying on the floor, exhausted from laughing.

'That's what I want the audience to think about when they see my version of the story,' Ms Robinson went on. 'And before I tell you who's playing what, a word of warning – I'll be using every single one of you, so if you don't get a proper part, it doesn't mean you won't be working your little socks off!'

There were more giggles at this, and a quickening of interest. Maze and Summer tossed their long hair and nudged each other smugly.

'First of all, it won't hang together without a really good narrator. As you'll see when you get your copies of the Carla Robinson version, there are places where I split up the bits of storytelling. But there has to be a main voice – Summer Watson.'

Maze let out a dramatic gasp; everyone had been so sure that Summer would be Alice. And Maze had fancied the main narrator for herself, to the point of deciding what she would wear.

Ha-ha, serves them both right.

Emily's gaze drifted to the darkening sky outside the big windows. For the first time since Holly died, she was glad it was Friday. She couldn't wait to get back to Barkstone Bygones to talk more about Smockeroon. Her own night had been disappointingly uneventful, but perhaps Ruth had seen something (or someone) else.

She listened with half an ear while Ms Robinson gave out the rest of the cast list.

'The White Rabbit – well, that has to be Martha Bishop, after her stunning performance in class the other day. The Red Queen – Maze Miller, I think you'll enjoy shouting "Off with their heads!"'

Everyone laughed at this, including Maze; both Maze and Summer were coming round to being pleased about the parts they had been given, but they were wild to know who would be playing Alice.

'And finally, the moment you've all been waiting for.' Ms Robinson made a noise like a drum roll. 'Ladies and – er – ladies, the part of Alice will be played by Emily Harding.'

It took Emily several seconds to hear her own name, and to realise that the entire class was gaping at her in obvious surprise.

Someone muttered, 'Who?'

Her cheeks burned. She looked over at Maze, and Maze looked back at her as if they had never met, with a horrible mixture of pity and scorn that made Emily's stomach curdle.

She had never been so glad to hear the bell.

'Just a minute!' Ms Robinson called. 'You all have

copies of my brilliant script – learn as many lines as you can!'

The day was over. There was a burst of talking, and a rush to the stage, where they had piled their coats and backpacks.

'Hey, well done!' Martha gave her a friendly nudge. 'You'll be fantastic as Alice.'

'Thanks,' Emily said automatically, her head still spinning with the shock of it. 'I'm glad you're the White Rabbit.'

Maze and Summer were muttering behind her, hardly even bothering to lower their voices.

Emily caught the words: '. . . of course she can't act. It's just because her sister died.'

Maze hissed, 'Shhh!'

'Don't you shush me – you said it yourself!'

Emily couldn't stop the painful rush of tears and had to pretend she was fiddling with her bag so nobody would see her face. Maze had been her closest friend. She had known Holly and Bluey, and how special they were, and now she was talking like a stranger.

The hall was emptying. Ms Robinson lingered beside the stage to gather up the stray pages of her

script. Emily hurriedly wiped her eyes and went to
help her.

'Thanks,' Ms Robinson said. 'I hope I didn't give
you too much of a shock just now.'

'Do you really think I can play Alice?'

'Of course! You'll be just right.'

'It's just that I've never really done any acting
before. And I might be rubbish.'

Ms Robinson gave her a look that was sharp, but
also kind. 'Oh, I see what this is – you think I gave you
the main part out of pity, because of Holly?'

Emily nodded, her throat aching again.

'Well, you can put that out of your head right
now. I'm not rewarding you for being related to
a dead person. And it's not because you've got
blonde hair, either – I was a wonderful black Alice
when I was at school. It was a major inspiration
for Tableland.'

'You played Tableland with Lenny, didn't you?'

'So you were listening after all. I never know how
much you're taking in. Yes, it was our favourite game.'
Ms Robinson shoved the last of the papers into her big
bag. 'I gave you the part of Alice because the audience
needs her to be someone they can identify with,

75

someone who can take them on the journey through the story.' She chuckled softly. 'Someone who's never been in an ad for B&Q.'

Six

TROUBLE IN
POINTED END

THE DOORBELL RANG AT half past nine, while Emily and her parents were watching *Masterchef* on television.

It was Ruth. 'Sorry to bother you so late – could I borrow Emily for a moment? I need her help with something.' She was trying to sound breezy and jolly but she was breathless, and her sagging brown cardigan was buttoned in the wrong holes. 'Emily, would you mind?'

Until then, it had been a very quiet Friday afternoon and evening. When Holly was alive, Emily had spent most of her Fridays with Maze. But Maze was at Summer's house, and her former best friend was left to doze on the sofa between her silent mother and father.

The panicky look in Ruth's eyes woke Emily like a rush of cold air. The moment they were outside on the front path, she said, 'You've seen something!'

Ruth stopped pretending to be jolly and clutched at Emily's hand. 'I need you to tell me you can see it too.'

'See what?'

'Oh crikey – wait just a minute, let me get my breath . . .' She halted a few feet away from her back door, panting as if she had been running. 'I was upstairs in the sitting room and I swear I wasn't asleep – and then all of a sudden— Emily, what's going on?' Her voice dropped to a fearful whisper. 'Why am I being haunted by my son's old toys?'

'Toys can't haunt people,' Emily said. 'They don't have ghosts.'

A shiver ran through her; even as she said it, she wondered if the Bluey who lived in Deep Smockeroon counted as a ghost.

'OK, I'm ready now.' Ruth squared her shoulders bravely and opened her back door. 'Come up as quietly as you can. I don't want to scare them off.'

The staircase in the ancient house was narrow and uneven. Emily followed Ruth, her heart fluttering with excitement. Inside the sitting room someone was talking – she couldn't make out the words – and then there was a burst of cheering. Ruth opened the door with extra care, as if she expected it to bite her.

The small sitting room was crowded with toys. They filled the sofa and the armchair, the top of the bookcase and the windowsill. There were bears of all shapes and colours, penguins large and small, several cuddly dinosaurs, a couple of giraffes and the soft puffin from the children's corner at the bookshop. It was an extraordinary sight – these squashed and battered creatures fidgeting, laughing, whispering to each other. Emily had to blink several times before she recognised the toys who had held their choir practice in her bedroom. None of them took the slightest notice of the two humans.

'You see?' whispered Ruth.

Hugo, perched on a cushion, was finishing off a speech, one flipper raised dramatically. 'And if it won't go by itself, we'll have to throw things at it and tear its house down!' (More cheers). 'As your newly elected mayor, I will send that rascal a clear message – we don't want your sort in Pointed End!'

All the toys cheered loudly.

'Hear hear!' said Sister Pretty.

'Can I take the bag off now?' asked Sister Toop.

'I suppose so, if you're careful not to look too beautiful.'

Emily knelt down on the carpet, to get closer to the toys. 'Hi, Hugo.'

'Ah, Emily!' Hugo said. 'You just missed my speech, but I'll send you a copy. Hello, Ruth!'

Ruth's lips moved soundlessly and her eyes bulged with amazement.

'More humans!' snapped Sister Pretty. 'You know I don't like humans! How did we get here, anyway?'

'It's that door again,' Smiffy said. 'I bet that's how you-know-who sneaked in!'

This set a wave of agitation through the toys.

Emily asked, 'Who's you-know-who?'

'Settle down, everybody!' shouted Hugo, his short, round body swelling importantly. 'Let me explain. We're the Pointed End Neighbourhood Watch, and we were having an emergency meeting.'

'But that's for guarding against crime!' Emily's dad was in the Barkstone Neighbourhood Watch, and she knew their meetings were mostly about things like security lights. 'Toys can't be criminals – can they?'

'Certainly not!' Hugo said briskly. 'The emergency is that a horrible toad has moved into our nice village and we were voting to chuck it out.'

The toys murmured and muttered.

'It's evil!' someone squeaked angrily.

'It's smelly!' someone else called out.

Smiffy said, 'And it's brought a banned substance into Smockeroon!'

'Hang on . . .' Emily's head was swimming; now the soft bear sounded like her headmistress talking about drugs. 'What banned substance?'

All together, the toys shouted, 'SADNESS!'

'Of course,' Ruth murmured, almost to herself.

'But you left a message for the Sturvey,' said Emily. 'Hasn't it done anything?'

'No,' said Hugo briskly. 'I haven't heard back from the Sturvey – I don't know why. That phone must be playing up. So I decided to put it in writing.'

'Good idea,' said Ruth. 'What's the address?'

'Just "The Sturvey, Deepest Smockeroon",' said Smiffy. 'Please don't think we're being mean about all toads – I know some really nice ones. But this toad is evil.'

There was a sudden surge of glittering light,

so bright that Emily and Ruth had to cover their eyes; when they could look again, the toys had vanished. It was just the two of them in an empty sitting room.

A single sheet of paper floated gently towards the floor. Ruth snatched it in mid-air and held it out so that they could both read it.

PerTIsHUN to the STURveY!
GeT RID OF thE EVIL TOAD!

'Dear old Hugo,' Ruth said quietly. 'His terrible spelling made Danny laugh so much!'

Emily said, 'I hope the message gets through this time. That black toad doesn't belong in Smockeroon.'

What if it hurts Bluey?

'And now the writing has disappeared – look!' Ruth held up what was now a blank piece of paper. 'What on earth is going on? Here we both are, wide awake and not crazy. So it must be some form of . . . magic.'

'Magic!' The word made Emily's pulse jump. It meant that anything was possible. For a fraction of a second she remembered Holly so vividly that she could almost reach out and touch her warm, smooth hand.

You're so near – if only I knew where to look.

'I don't know what else to call it. Do you understand all the stuff about the broken door? Is it just one broken door – or lots of them?'

'Hugo says it's one door, at the bottom of his garden, which keeps taking them to the wrong places, so they never know where they'll be coming out next,' Emily said. 'Could it be my fault, because I started dreaming about the toys? Or did I dream about them because they were there already?'

Downstairs in the shop, three antique clocks began to chime.

'You'd better get home now, before your parents think I've kidnapped you.' Ruth rubbed her hair distractedly. 'But please come straight round and let me know if you see anything else, even if it's only a dream. The shop's usually quiet on Saturday afternoons.'

'We'll probably be out tomorrow afternoon,' Emily said. 'It's the Autumn Fair at the hospital.'

★

Holly had spent a lot of time at Bottleton General Hospital. It was a place they all knew only too well. Mum had often stayed there when Holly was very ill, sleeping beside her on a hard camp bed. Emily had practically grown up there – she remembered learning to crawl along the endless corridors, and riding her tricycle across the gravelled paths outside.

Every year, the hospital held a big autumn fair to raise money. Emily had always looked forward to this event. There was a live band, a bouncy castle and great food, and Holly had loved sitting with Mum behind the tombola stall – she couldn't see the strings of fairy lights, but she had been able to feel the thud-thud-thud of the music played by the band.

Mum wasn't involved with all the planning this year, but it never crossed Emily's mind that they would not be going to the Autumn Fair. Only yesterday her mother had been talking brightly about 'popping in for a cup of tea'.

'But I can't do it,' Emily heard her saying to Dad on Saturday morning. 'I know I won't be able to bear it without her. I'm not ready to go back to the place where she died.'

'I know, I know,' Dad said. 'I'm sure Em will understand if we give it a miss.'

They were using what Emily thought of as their 'private' voices – dark and soaked with sadness, no matter how hard they pretended everything was fine when they were talking to her.

She assured them that she didn't mind missing the Autumn Fair. It was mostly true. Maze and Summer would be there and Emily didn't fancy hearing any more snide remarks about her acting.

But it made for another very dull Saturday.

Emily spent the morning updating her report in the Bluey book.

The black toad has invaded Smockeroon.
Hugo is the new mayor of Pointed End.
The Sturvey is not answering messages.

In the afternoon, suddenly longing to get out of the silent house, she went to Pauline's to buy a bag of rice for supper (Dad was making his vegetarian chilli con carne – in the old days the fart siren would have gone berserk).

Ruth had said the shop would be quiet, but the

pavement outside Barkstone Bygones was blocked by three young mums with buggies, and another mum was carefully backing another buggy out of the door. Emily peered through the window and saw Ruth at the till, wrapping something for a man who was carrying a toddler in a frame on his back.

Ruth saw Emily and beckoned to her to come inside. 'Would you get me a brown loaf and some tea bags and milk? It's been so frantic today that I haven't had a chance to do any shopping.' She added, raising her eyebrows significantly, 'And I've made rather an interesting discovery.'

Ruth had seen something else. Emily hurried to Pauline's shop, now really glad she hadn't gone to the Autumn Fair. Magic was far more exciting.

The customers had gone by the time she got back.

'Thanks, Emily.' Ruth was sitting behind the till, writing busily in her 'Sales' book. 'It's been an odd sort of morning. One customer after another, and all squeezing in with their enormous baby buggies – more like Waterloo Station than a small antique shop!'

Emily sat down in the old armchair beside the wood burner. The sagging cushions were blissfully comfortable and she liked the musty smell of the threadbare linen covers. 'Did they buy anything?'

'Yes – all of them! I've never seen anything like it. Three Staffordshire figurines, both boxes of Minton tiles, one engraving of the ruins of Bottleton Abbey – and the hideous pokerwork fire screen that I thought I'd never get rid of!'

'What was your discovery?'

Before Ruth could reply, yet another customer came in – another mum with a toddler in a buggy.

She said, 'My little boy wants to wave to the bear.'

Notty was in his usual place on the shelf behind Ruth, between the two large clocks. The toddler squawked happily and flapped his little fist.

'He's a popular bear today,' Ruth said. 'Everyone wants to wave to him!'

'And while I'm in here, could I look at the candlesticks in the window?'

Ruth and the customer went over to the window, turning their backs on the buggy. The toddler chuckled and waved and tried to say 'Bear!'

And then Emily saw something that made her squeak aloud with shock.

Up on his shelf, Notty was *waving back*.

Seven

RESEARCH

'WAVING?' RUTH STARED AT the disintegrating old bear. 'Are you sure?'

'He waved both his arms,' Emily said. 'And then he stood up and did a little dance – I was so scared the lady would turn round and see him!'

The three working clocks had chimed five and the shop was now closed.

'Well, that explains a lot,' Ruth said. 'I was wondering why I've been visited by every toddler in town, and it's because my mother's old bear is waving and dancing and generally showing off to them!' She patted Notty's head. 'What's going on, old bear?'

The old bear was a toy again, a heap of stitches and sawdust.

'He's gone,' said Emily. 'But his body's still here.

Does that mean he can choose when he comes to life? Or does the aliveness just come and go by itself?'

'I have absolutely no idea! And when I try to think about it my brain turns to mush. My guess would be that the power – or whatever – sort of flickers on and off for no reason, like the dodgy light on my upstairs landing. There's some sort of interference. I wish I could talk to Danny – his imagination was so good when it came to this sort of thing. He did once tell me a story about Hugo and Smiffy suddenly coming to life at his school, after a freak explosion in the science lab.'

Emily asked, 'What was your discovery?'

'Hmm?' Ruth was deep in thought.

'You said you'd made a discovery.'

'Oh, yes – I don't think it's particularly important, just something rather interesting.' She gave Emily a searching look. 'But I thought you'd be at the Autumn Fair.'

'Mum couldn't face it.'

'Fair enough.' Ruth took her bread, milk and teabags out of the shopping bag. 'It's too soon for her. Poor thing, she looks absolutely lost sometimes. She had fifteen years of looking after Holly twenty-four hours a day, and now she doesn't know what to do with herself.'

'She says she's forgotten how to sleep,' said Emily. 'She keeps waking up because she thinks Holly's calling to her.'

'Mothers get used to being needed.' Ruth let out a long sigh. 'When Danny died, it broke my heart that nobody needed me like that any more. I wasn't anybody's mother – it was like being made redundant.'

'But you'll always be Danny's mother.' Emily remembered what Ms Robinson had said about Holly always being her sister. 'Nothing can take that away.'

'I suppose you're right, and it's a much better way of looking at things.' She was smiling again. 'Anyway, I hope you don't mind too much about missing the fair.'

'Not really,' Emily said. 'It was only fun when Holly was there. And I'm sort of avoiding my former best friend.'

'You mean Maze Miller? Don't tell me you two have fallen out!'

'We haven't argued, or anything. She just acts as if she didn't know me. It's really weird.'

'That's a shame,' Ruth said. 'But don't take it personally. People can be very strange when you've had a death in the family. One of my closest friends stopped speaking to me when I lost Daniel. If she saw me in the street she ran away.'

'Why?'

'I think my sadness frightened her. She got over it eventually, and so will Ms Miller – she'll have to notice you when you're both in the school play, won't she?'

'I suppose so.' Emily hoped this was true. She missed having someone of her own age to tell things to.

Ruth took the ancient bear down from his shelf. 'I'll keep this guy where I can see him this evening – if I leave him in the shop I'll worry that he's cavorting about in the window. Are you sure you saw him moving?'

'Yes, and the baby definitely saw him too.'

'Is the magic somehow leaking out of Smockeroon?' Ruth absently tidied a loose thread on one of Notty's wonky old ears. 'I can't stop wondering why this is happening to us – you and me in particular, I mean.' She gave a sudden snort of laughter. 'Good old Hugo – it's so nice to meet him properly after all these years! Tell you what, since you're not at the hospital fair, give your dad his bag of rice and then come back here.'

'OK.' Emily was longing to talk more about the magic – what else could you call it? And if Ruth had met Hugo, perhaps she could somehow climb through that broken door and meet Bluey, who would lead her to Holly. She hurried back to her house, shoved the bag of rice at Dad and told him she would be next door.

'At Maze's?' Dad was reading the paper at the kitchen table, with a strangely sleepy look in his eyes.

'No, Dad – Maze doesn't live next door! I'm at Ruth's.'

Ruth was in her kitchen when Emily got back. There was a pile of tattered old books on the table, and Notty, Hugo and Smiffy sat at one end of the dresser.

Emily patted each toy's head affectionately. 'They're like grubby cushions now – it's really weird to think of them moving and talking.'

'And yet we both know what we saw.' Ruth sat down at the table, moving most of the book pile to the floor so that she and Emily could see each other properly. 'For some reason, you and I are having the same hallucinations – if that's what they are. And after you'd gone home last night, I found out something very interesting.'

'Did you see something? Did they move again?'

'You might not like this,' Ruth said, 'but I suddenly remembered where I'd heard the word "Smockeroon".'

'You must've heard me telling stories to Holly.' Emily's pulse quickened with a strange sense of mingled dread and excitement. 'I made up that word.'

'You didn't make it up.' Ruth picked up the thick book at the top of the pile. 'John Staples did.'

'But—' This couldn't be true; Smockeroon belonged to her and to Holly, not some old writer from history.

'It's not in any of his novels,' Ruth said. 'It's from his childhood.' The book was called *Dreamer of Dreams: A Life of John Staples*. She opened it to show Emily a black-and-white photograph of three children – two boys in sailor suits, and a little girl in a white lace dress. 'John, William and Mary Staples, taken in 1908, under that famous tree. "Smockeroon" was the name John invented for the stories they told each other about their toys.'

She turned the page to another old photograph of

93

three antique toys – a tin monkey, a donkey and a small, light-coloured bear. The caption underneath said, 'Blokey, Mokey and Figinda Faraway.'

'But I don't understand!' Emily was bewildered, and a little scared. 'I've never heard of those toys, so how did I hear about Smockeroon?'

'It's perfectly possible that you heard the word somewhere,' Ruth said. 'But it doesn't explain how you met Hugo and Smiffy. It doesn't explain half of what we've seen – it only increases the mystery. I wanted to do some serious research, so I began by collecting every book I had about people who enter imaginary worlds.'

Emily looked properly at the pile of books.

Some were familiar – *Alice in Wonderland. The Lion, the Witch and the Wardrobe. Winnie-the-Pooh.* And some were strange, like the tatty old volume called *At the Back of the North Wind*, by someone called George MacDonald.

'But I didn't get anywhere,' Ruth went on, 'until I remembered the Staples connection, and the very sad story of his childhood. As you know, the family lived in the house that's now next door to the house of your ex-friend Maze. In those days, at the beginning of the twentieth century, it was surrounded by fields. Their father was a stern old Victorian type with grey whiskers, and their mother died when Mary was born – that happened more often in those days. They weren't allowed to see other children and they didn't go to school.'

'Wasn't that illegal?' Emily often wished she didn't have to go to school.

'Not in those days. They had a teacher who came in every morning and made them shout their times tables while doing Swedish exercises.'

'Ugh!' Even Hatty Catty was preferable to that.

'The children escaped into their invented world of Smockeroon, telling each other elaborate stories about the adventures of their toys. Just like you and Holly.'

'And you and Daniel, with the Land of Neverendings.' Emily had got over being dismayed and was now very curious. 'You didn't have the same name for it, but it's obviously the same place, and it's like our imaginations are leaking into each other and getting mixed up.'

'It gets stranger,' Ruth said, 'and sadder. When he was only nine, John was sent off to boarding school. Before he left, he and his brother invented a spell so that they could meet every night in their dreams.' She added, 'In Smockeroon.'

'Did it work?' Emily was still waiting, and longing, to dream about Holly.

'John always swore that it worked beautifully,' Ruth said. 'Even when he was old and famous. Night after night, the two lonely boys comforted their sad hearts by dreaming that they were together in their own enchanted forest.'

Emily suddenly knew why the boys had been so sad; it dropped into her mind all at once, though she had no idea where it came from. 'Mary died, didn't she?'

'Yes, poor little thing,' Ruth said. 'They all had scarlet fever and Mary died of it. She was only six.'

'That's awful.'

'How small a part of time they share, that are so wondrous sweet and fair.'

'Sorry?'

'It's a poem,' Ruth said. 'Death makes you understand all the famous poems about death and dying. It's the same when you fall in love.'

'I'm glad I had Holly for longer than six years,' Emily said. 'I wouldn't have nearly so much to remember.'

'I must admit, the story made me cry, though it happened so long ago. After the fever, the Staples house had to be thoroughly cleaned and disinfected. A lot of things had to be burned – including all the children's toys.'

Like Bluey.

Dead sisters and burnt toys.

'But there was a story a few years ago,' Ruth said. 'Someone found a letter from John Staples when he was an old man, in which he claimed that he'd saved his chief toys from the fire and hidden them somewhere safe. He didn't say where.'

'Do you think he's the reason this is all happening?'

'Well, apart from the fact that both our houses are close to his, there is one very obvious connection between us. We've all lost our darlings. And we'd all give the world to see them again, in the place where we were happiest.'

Emily felt a prickle of excitement.

John and his brother found a way into Smockeroon.

'We need that spell!'

The days wouldn't be nearly so bad, if I knew I could dream of Holly and Bluey every night.

There was a loud knock on the back door. Dad had

come to fetch Emily for supper. 'It's waiting on the table. And I must say, I'm rather proud of it.'

'Hi, Rob,' Ruth said. 'What's all that stuff coming out of your sleeve?'

Emily saw that one sleeve of Dad's denim jacket was coated with little coloured specks that scattered every time he moved. She picked one off the table and tasted it. 'Hundreds and thousands? I thought you were cooking vegetarian chilli.'

'Was I?' Dad was smiling, with a strange, faraway look in his eyes. 'Chilli? No, I've made a big red jelly with custard and cream and hundreds and thousands.'

'Jelly?' Emily hadn't eaten jelly for years, but jelly had featured in many of her stories about Smockeroon. The toys had a sport called jelly jumping; Bluey had been the world champion.

'I don't know what got into me,' Dad said. 'I forgot to make anything else.'

Ruth looked at him sharply. 'You made pudding, but you forgot the dinner?' She raised her eyebrows at Emily; it was obvious to them both that this had to be more of what could only be called magic.

'Oh, dear.' He blinked several times. 'We'd better

get a takeaway – why on earth did I do that? I don't even like jelly!'

Dad took Emily's hand on the way home, something he hadn't done for a long time. His fingers were warm and strong.

In the darkness she heard him laughing softly. 'Nothing but jelly for supper – she would've loved that, wouldn't she?'

'Yes,' Emily said. 'You'd have to give her jelly wobbles.' This was the special, wobbly kind of tickling he had invented to make Holly smile.

'Sometimes, when I'm cooking,' Dad said, 'I pretend she's still here. I pretend that she's behind me and I only have to turn round to see her.'

He gave her hand a squeeze, and Emily squeezed back.

Eight

BATTLE OF
THE BEDROOM

'WILLIES AND BALLS,' the silvery voice said. 'All over my back, in black marker pen that won't wash off.'

'Oh, don't talk to me about willies!' exclaimed another high voice. 'My owner's brother drew a willy on me – in bright purple ink!'

'My scars are in words, not pictures,' a deeper voice said. '"Milk, milk, lemonade, round the corner chocolate's made." Well, you all know it. My owner thought it was hilarious.'

Emily opened her eyes. Though the lamp was off, her room was filled with that pale, unearthly light that the toys brought with them into the hard world, and she felt a surge of happiness.

'Hugo? Smiffy?' She sat up.

'They're not here today.' Sister Pretty popped out from behind a fold in the duvet. 'This is the new self-help group I've started, for toys who have been scribbled on. Soft bears and penguins couldn't possibly understand – it makes us so dreadfully sad!'

'Sad, in Smockeroon? But that's not possible!'

Emily switched on the lamp to get a better view of the knobbly, grubby crowd at the end of her bed – the two nuns, plus seven more Barbies, and two military action figures. She was starting to get used to the oddness of it all, but it was still incredibly odd to see these strange toys turning their plastic heads to look at her.

One of the Barbies asked, 'What's the human doing here?'

'Frankly, I don't know,' said Sister Pretty. 'It's all very puzzling – try to ignore her.'

There was a muffled shriek and someone fell off the bed.

'Not again!' Sister Pretty rolled her eyes impatiently. 'Sister Toop, stop fooling about! You're supposed to be handing round the refreshments!'

'Maybe you should let her take the bag off her head,' Emily suggested. 'She can't see anything.'

'Oh, all right! But I'll have to ask the group, in case she makes them jealous.'

'You're the only one who gets jealous,' one of the other Barbies said. 'We're all fine with it.'

The unfairly beautiful Toop lay on the rug, surrounded by little dots like the lights on a Christmas tree; Emily leaned out of bed to look more closely, and saw that they were tiny cakes that vanished in a puff of glitter when she tried to touch them. She picked up Toop, put her back on the duvet and pulled the bag off her head.

'Thanks, Emily!' gasped Sister Toop.

'Look, what's going on?' One of the action figures stood up angrily. 'I thought we were in your back garden in Pointed End, not some human's bedroom!'

'Oh, don't worry about Emily,' Sister Pretty said breezily. 'She's the nice sort of human.'

'If she's so nice, why is her room full of empty toys?' He pointed to the top shelf where Emily kept all the old soft toys that people had given her since she was a baby.

She looked up at them with a stab of guilt; she'd liked them but never really played with them. The scribbled-on soldier called them 'empty' and she knew what he meant. They were just so much fur and stuffing, without a spark of magic.

'Lots of humans have empty toys,' said Sister Pretty. 'It only means they haven't been imagined yet. But Emily imagined Bluey.'

'Bluey? That's different.' He sat down again.

'Is he a friend of yours?' Emily had a sudden, painful longing to see Bluey in his old place on Holly's wheelchair.

'Yes, he gave me a cheery wave this morning, in the queue at the post office.'

Emily didn't remember any post offices in Smockeroon – but before she could ask more questions, there was a sudden loud POP, like a large balloon bursting, and a cloud of thick pink candyfloss smoke appeared on the carpet. The smoke melted away to reveal the little striped tent – and Hugo and Smiffy.

'This is the last straw,' said Sister Pretty, her plastic face denting into a scowl. 'What are they doing here?'

'Come along, everybody!' Hugo shouted importantly. 'Find your partners!'

The tent flap opened and out came two soft penguins – followed by two more, and then two

103

more, until Emily's bedroom floor was crowded with toy penguins, all honking and shouting and milling about, their long beaks busily opening and shutting.

'Shhh – you'll wake up my parents!' She jumped out of bed, with a vague idea of cutting Mum and Dad off on the landing before they could get into her room and see the toys; she hadn't a clue how she would explain the racket.

The landing was empty, however, and her parents were still securely asleep behind their bedroom door. Emily stepped carefully across a carpet of soft penguins and climbed back into bed to enjoy the entertainment.

Oh, how silly this is – and how I've missed silliness!

'We'll start with a Penguin Polka. Smiffy, switch the music on when I wave my flipper.'

'OK, Hugo.' Smiffy, the only non-penguin in the group, was fiddling with half of an old Weetabix packet that had been painted to look like a radio.

'EXCUSE ME!' yelled Sister Pretty, running to the end of Emily's bed. 'What are you doing here? This is an outrage! Go away at once – that frightful toad is making everybody so rude.'

The penguins saw her and broke out in a noisy storm of honks and shrieks.

'What are you doing here?' demanded Hugo. 'This is the ballroom of the Penguin Society, and you are interrupting our dancing club.'

The Barbie nun stamped her foot. 'Nonsense! We've slipped into Emily's bedroom again – and you are interrupting our group therapy for the scribbled!'

'Emily's bedroom?' Hugo looked around furiously. 'Oh, labels! I booked that ballroom until six!'

'HOW DARE YOU SWEAR AT ME!' shrieked Sister Pretty. 'It's that wretched broken door at the bottom of your garden – I thought this was the Bratz-and-Barbies Social Club!'

'Excuse me.' Emily was suddenly gripped by a new and amazing idea. 'If the broken door leads into my bedroom, does that mean I could get into Smockeroon from this side?'

'Alive human beings can't come in, except in their imagination,' said Sister Pretty, kindly but firmly. 'It's just not possible.'

'OK. Can you show me how you get back to Smockeroon?' Maybe she did not need John's spell after all; Sister Pretty said it was impossible, but she was only a plastic doll.

'Through the little tent, dear, where the light's coming from.'

'Oh.' The striped tent was tiny – far too small for a human to get into.

But it's worth a try. The rabbit hole wasn't too small for Alice.

She watched the toys carefully, waiting for the moment they all decided to leave. It happened at the end of the dance. The penguins bowed to each other and then neatly hopped into the striped tent. Sister Pretty and her self-help group jumped off the bed to stand at the end of the queue.

Emily knelt down on the rug behind the toys. From her crouching position, she saw the tent-flaps and the calm white light that shone, bright and steady, from the inside. The queue was moving fast. If she kept close she could get her head into the tent before the toys disappeared, and that might be enough.

Let this work! Why shouldn't it work?

Alice found a bottle that said 'Drink Me' and it made her shrink – please let me find something like that!

She dived after the last toy, and for one breathless moment her eyes were dazzled by a great burst of light—

And then it was morning, and Emily woke up to find herself stretched face down on the rug, one hand reaching out at nothing.

★

'You're not at primary school now,' Mrs Lewis said. 'This is where education gets serious. I expect mature behaviour and hard work. I know you all think the exams are far away in the distant future, but the preparation starts here. And this lot of homework is shoddy and slapdash and a general disgrace.'

Mrs Lewis was so old that her hair was white, and so tough that even the headmistress seemed slightly scared of her. There was no question of writing anything in the Bluey book during one of her classes. She was the sort of teacher who could see your thoughts.

'Some of you haven't made any effort at all. You obviously haven't been paying the slightest bit of attention in class (Maze Miller, for God's sake STOP TALKING). Well, I'm warning all you daydreamers (yes, Amber Frost and Emily Harding, I do mean you), there'll be no more drifting off during my lessons, thank you very much. And no more whispering or giggling, Martha Bishop.'

'Mrs Lewis is such a witch,' Martha said afterwards. 'I wasn't giggling – it's just the way my face looks. It's not my fault I was born with a giggly looking face.'

Martha had plumped down beside Emily at lunch. She had decided she was Emily's friend, refusing to be put off by her long silences or her obsessive scribbling in the Bluey book, and Emily had found it impossible not to like her.

'I was hoping you'd be at the hospital fair on Saturday,' Martha said. 'I looked everywhere for you. But my mum said I shouldn't be surprised that you weren't there. She said it probably made you too sad because of your sister.'

This was a bit tactless, but Emily didn't mind – Martha's squirrel chatter was never painful.

'Oh, it was so funny – I won a prize in the raffle, a six-pack of beer! Everyone laughed when I went up to get it, and I had to sell it to my uncle. My mum said I had to spend the money at the fair because it was for charity – so I bought a very sweet little bear from the toy stall.'

'A bear?'

'I know, I know, I'm far too old for soft toys! But it was that or bath salts. And there was just something about this bear.' Martha opened her backpack and Emily saw a small teddy bear with pale yellow fur. 'Her name's Pippa.'

'But that's— I mean—' Emily had to stop herself blurting it out, but she had met Pippa before.

'I had a really silly dream about her last night,' Martha said. 'All I can remember is something about sewing.'

'Seams,' said Emily.

'Yes, that's it – seams.'

Martha didn't have a clue that she'd bought herself one of the famous Seam-Rite Girls.

Nine

EXPERIMENT

'IT'S MY BIRTHDAY IN TWO WEEKS TIME, at the beginning of half-term,' said Martha the next day, during lunch. 'And I'll be having a sleepover. It always has to be a sleepover – our house is in the middle of nowhere.'

Martha lived on a farm a few miles outside Bottleton, where the real countryside began.

'I hope you can come, by the way.'

'I don't know. I think so.' Emily realised this sounded rude and quickly added, 'Thanks.' She had been thinking about Pippa, and how odd it was that Martha owned the little yellow Seam-Rite bear.

'I'll draw a map to show how you get there. I'll be asking quite a few people from my old primary school, but don't worry that you won't know anyone – the Ambers are coming.

'I love sleepovers,' said Amber Frost.

'I love parties full stop,' said Amber Jones.

The Ambers often appeared alongside Martha, and Emily was starting to notice them properly and enjoy their company. They shared a first name, but they were very different. Amber Frost was tall and skinny, with short brown hair that stood up in tufts and thick glasses, and a general air of dreaminess (she was the other daydreamer targeted by Mrs Lewis in her anti-daydreamer campaign). Amber Jones was short and stocky and lively, with pink cheeks and sparky dark eyes.

'And in case you're wondering about birthday presents,' Martha said, 'I genuinely like book tokens.'

'Book tokens? Seriously?' Amber Jones pulled a face. 'Wouldn't you rather get chocolate, or make-up, or something?'

'Seriously! I like to collect loads of book tokens for my birthday and for Christmas, and then I splurge the lot in one mad spending spree at the bookshop – last year I needed two plastic bags.'

It was the tail end of lunch break and they were in

the classroom, gathered around Martha's desk which was beside the radiator.

Emily had eaten her lunch at the same table as Maze, Summer and their show-offy gang, for the simple reason that all the other tables were full – and her former best friend had actually turned her back, as if Emily had done something wrong. She tried to remember what Ruth had said about people being frightened of too much sadness, but it had still been horrible, and she had run off to the empty classroom to cry.

But then Martha and the Ambers had appeared, too full of the birthday sleepover to notice anything else. And as the classroom filled up, everyone started talking about the play. They were about to have another rehearsal. To her slight surprise, Emily was enjoying the experience of playing Alice – maybe because they had so much in common. When Alice fell down the rabbit hole and came out in Wonderland, Emily imagined how she would feel if she ever managed to get to Smockeroon, and Ms Robinson said she was 'very convincing'.

'I've learned all my lines,' Martha said. 'Not very hard, when all I say is, "I'm late!"'

'I think I know mine,' said Amber Frost, who was playing the Caterpillar. She nudged Emily. 'What about you?'

'I'm getting there,' Emily said. (In fact she was word-perfect; it was easy to learn a few lines when her time wasn't taken up with Holly and Maze.)

'This whole Alice thing is doing my head in,' Martha said, with one of her trademark giggles. 'Last night, I had this ridiculous dream that I was at a weird tea party – but instead of the Dormouse and the Mad Hatter, it was the little yellow bear I got at the hospital fair. How mad is that?'

The Ambers laughed at this, and Emily tried to join in, though her every sense prickled with alarm.

So Martha was seeing things from Smockeroon.

★

'Well, that certainly sounds like Smockeroon,' Ruth said. 'The magic must be positively flowing through that broken door. It's getting everywhere!'

It was Thursday again and Ruth was in an odd mood, distracted and a bit furtive, as if she were hiding something.

'Have you seen anything else? Has Notty been moving again?'

'No, it's been pretty quiet today,' said Ruth. 'I've been doing some more research.'

'And?'

'I did find something. It's rather complicated – hang on, we can't talk properly until I've closed up.'

She turned the sign on the door from 'Open' to 'Closed' and they went into the kitchen. It was messier than ever. There were more old books piled on the table, and the top of the dresser was covered with what looked like grass from the garden and small clumps of soil.

'You can laugh if you like,' Ruth said, 'but the long and short of it is that I've been trying to cast a spell.'

'Sorry?'

'You know – like a witch.'

'You've found John's spell!' Emily cried out eagerly. 'The spell that made him dream about Smockeroon!'

'Well, yes.'

'Have you tried it? Did it work?'

'Not so fast – yes, I've found the spell, and put together most of the ingredients.' Ruth sat down at the table, absently opening a large bag of Minstrels.

'I've been trying to find out as much as possible about the Staples children. The stuff that's available online isn't enough, and neither are the biographies – but I suddenly remembered that I bought the collected letters of John Staples a couple of years ago. They were in three gigantic volumes and too damp to sell, so I stashed them in the cellar. Last night I went down there – with a torch, and destroying my tights – to fetch the one with the letters he wrote as a child.'

'And the spell was in a letter he wrote to his brother? What was his name?'

'Yes – William. Way ahead of me, as usual.' Ruth opened a thick book, wafting a strong smell of damp and mould across the table. 'The ingredients are pretty straightforward – grass and soil from the garden, plus a drop of blood.'

Emily shivered. 'Real blood?'

'My blood,' said Ruth grimly, 'assuming I'm the chief spellbinder, which is what John called himself.' She read from the book:

Take ten five-centimetre blades of grass and one teaspoon of garden soil. Put them in a saucepan

115

with a pint of water. When the water starts to boil,
the chief spellbinder must prick his thumb with a
needle and squeeze a large drop of blood into the
mixture. At that exact moment, the chief spellbinder
and the deputy spellbinder must chant in unison –
'To Smockeroon! Smockeroon! Smockeroon!'

She added, 'I haven't done it yet. The spell needs two people so I waited for you. And quite honestly, I'm still in two minds about going through with it.'

'But we must go through with it!' This was a huge breakthrough; Emily could not bear to miss any chance to get to Smockeroon. 'I'll be the chief whatsit if you don't like the blood – but we can't turn back now!'

'Oh, no.' Ruth was suddenly firm and grown-up. 'You're not shedding any blood! That's my responsibility. But I don't think it'll work.'

'You don't know that. What happens after the blood goes in?'

'You take a teaspoon of the mixture, just before you go to bed. You lie down flat on your back with your arms by your side and recite the rhyme.' Ruth read it out from the book.

Magic mountains, valleys deep,
Let me see you when I sleep!
Take me to that meadow sweet
Where my toys and I can meet!'

They were both quiet for a moment. Emily ran through the rhyme in her mind. 'Is that all? I expected something more complicated.'

'Me too – but John said it worked.'

'Shall we try it tonight?'

'Not so fast,' Ruth said. 'I think I'd better do this alone, at least for the first time.'

'Why?' This was disappointing when Emily had just got her hopes up. 'Is the recipe poisonous, or something?'

'Oh no, the ingredients are quite safe on their own. It's the magic element that worries me. We know so little about it. And think how it would look if anything bad happened to you.' Ruth was as serious as anyone can be while crunching Minstrels. 'I couldn't possibly explain it to your parents.'

'They don't need to know!'

'They'll know if it all goes wrong,' said Ruth. 'Give them a break. They've already lost one child.'

'Come on, it's not going to kill me!'

'Emily, we've seen enough to know the "magic" is real. We have to treat this spell with the utmost respect.'

'But it might not work with only one person doing it.'

'Maybe not, and if nothing happens at all we'll have to think again. But I want to be absolutely sure.'

'Well, OK.' Though she was annoyed to be left out of the experiment, Emily had to admit that she saw the sense in this; it was horrible to think of Mum and Dad being left behind in their empty house, with only memories of the girls they had loved so much. 'But you'll be OK, won't you?' She was suddenly worried about Ruth; it was nearly as horrible to think of her empty shop. And Smockeroon no longer seemed such a safe place now that the black toad had broken in.

'Oh, I'll be fine,' said Ruth. 'I'm a tough old boot.'

'So . . . what do we do first?'

'You're serious, aren't you?' Ruth sighed, but she was smiling. 'Well, all right, you can start by sorting out those blades of grass, and I'll sterilize the needle in some boiling water.'

Emily used her ruler to measure ten five-centimetre

blades of grass, which she laid out neatly on a clean plate. Ruth measured out a pint of water and poured it into a saucepan on the stove. She then dropped in the blades of grass and a teaspoon of the nicest-looking soil from the garden.

'Now we wait for it to boil.'

They had both started to giggle, but only because they were excited.

It was ages before the first bubbles appeared in the pan. Ruth found her needle and held it in the steam from the electric kettle.

'Here goes – if you're squeamish, look away now – ouch!' She drove the needle into the top of her thumb, and they both watched the fat bead of blood falling into the boiling water. Together they chanted, 'To Smockeroon! Smockeroon! Smockeroon!'

They had stopped giggling now. In breathless silence, they gazed into the saucepan.

'Well, that's it,' said Ruth, 'our first magic potion is now complete.'

At last, perilously close to Emily's mother coming back from work, the spell was finished. Their magic potion looked like nothing more than some faintly dirty water with a few bits of grass floating on the surface.

Could this dirty water really make Ruth dream about Smockeroon? Emily had a strong sense that it could; somehow, it looked powerful.

'Well, one little spoonful won't hurt me.' Ruth sniffed the mixture cautiously. 'Imagine if it works – just imagine!' Her eyes were bright with hope and longing. 'One glimpse of him in a dream would be enough!'

She was silenced by loud knocking on the back door.

'That's Mum,' Emily said. 'Good luck – tell me everything – and please be careful!'

Ten

INSIDE
THE SYCAMORES

EMILY COULDN'T RESIST trying out at least part of the spell when she went to bed – just in case some of the magic leaked out from next door. She switched off the lamp and lay on her back with her arms at her sides.

She whispered the rhyme:

Magic mountains, valleys deep,
Let me see you when I sleep!
Take me to that meadow sweet
Where the toys and I can meet!

I can see Holly if I want it hard enough.

Though she wasn't aware of falling asleep, Emily woke up in the middle of the night. She was beginning to recognise the particular feeling she got when she saw the toys – a surge of happiness so intense that it was like fear.

'Hugo?'

She looked for the little tent, but her room was dark and silent.

'Sister Pretty?'

There were noises downstairs in the sitting room – a mumble of voices, followed by a burst of music. Emily got out of bed, pulled on her dressing gown and went out onto the landing. Her parents were fast asleep; she could hear Dad snoring behind their bedroom door. She tiptoed downstairs. Coloured lights spilled into the hall, like the essence of a thousand Christmases.

The sitting room was filled with dazzling colours, so bright that Emily had to half close her eyes for a few seconds before she could see anything properly.

The light was coming from the television, which had switched on by itself.

Toys' TV!

Giddy with joy, Emily dropped down on the sofa to watch. The jumble of coloured shapes on the screen was toys dancing against a background of trees, flowers and sunlight. Incredibly, she was looking into Smockeroon – and it was even more beautiful than she had imagined. Though there was no sign of Holly or Bluey, Emily knew they were there.

It's just like I told you – always summertime, unless it's Christmas!

The picture on the screen changed to a close-up of a large blue bottle, and a jaunty voice began to sing:

I was a bear with a terrible CORF,
I corfed so hard my ears blew ORF,
Till a kind friend told me what to do –
He said BEARCORF is the thing for you!

And then a smiling bear, who didn't seem at all self-conscious about the fact that she had a blob of old human's chewing-gum stuck to one cheek, took a spoonful of blue liquid from the bottle.

An advert for bears' cough medicine? That was crazy – toys didn't get coughs. Emily made a mental note to ask Ruth about Bearcorf and settled back more comfortably. The advertisements (there were a lot of these; the toys seemed to prefer them to actual programs) were hilarious.

'It's TREACLE WEEK at Pa Hank's
HOUSE OF SYRUP!'
'Get your party GOING – with a pie
that's for THROWING!'
'Do you have WHEELS? Banish those
embarrassing CREAKS with THOMPSON'S
OIL-OF-BUTTERSCOTCH!'

The colours were beautiful but the quality was dreadful – toys kept forgetting their words, and sometimes the theme tunes were just somebody humming.

'And now,' said the announcer, 'a change to the published programme. It was going to be the popular game show *Post Your Arms*, but the Sturvey banned it, saying the bank holiday 'Post Your Head' challenge was just too silly and the Smockeroon postal service couldn't cope with all the extra parcels.'

Emily had been feeling pleasantly dreamy, but she woke up when she caught the mention of the Sturvey.

If it can interfere with the TV, why can't it deal with the evil toad?

'Now a brand-new series,' the announcer went on,

'showing day-to-day life in an ordinary Smockeroon boarding house – *Inside The Sycamores*.'

'The Sycamores!' Emily sat bolt upright. This was beyond her wildest dreams – the famous boarding house.

The screen showed a dazzling summery garden and a heap of brightly coloured rubbish.

No, wait . . .

After a few seconds Emily saw that the messy structure of painted cardboard and sticky tape was not rubbish at all. This was The Sycamores itself, with its refined clientele and private jelly pond.

The picture changed to the face of a well-known penguin. 'Welcome to The Sycamores!'

'Hugo!' Emily gasped.

It was very strange indeed to see Hugo's look of astonishment in close-up. He frowned into the camera for a moment, then he smiled. 'Oh, hallo Emily.'

'You can see me?'

'Of course I can – you're on our television in the kitchen.'

'I'm on television?' This was even stranger. 'So are you – I mean, that's how I can see you.'

'Well, I'm glad you tuned in,' said Hugo. 'Now if you'll excuse me, I have to think of my audience. Ladies and gentlemen, my name is Hugo. I'm President of the Penguin Society and Mayor of Pointed End. The bobbly bear is my best friend Smiffy. When our owner left the hard world, we moved to Deep Smockeroon and decided to turn our beautiful mansion into a boarding house for independent toys like us— Good gracious!' The penguin suddenly looked off camera and his beak dropped open in amazement. 'This IS a surprise! How did you get here?'

The camera pulled back to show the whole room, and Emily nearly fell off the sofa. 'Ruth?'

It was an incredible sight. Ruth was sitting at a table, in a kitchen that had been decorated with clashing strips of flowered wrapping paper. Ruth was a human and much bigger than the toys, but somehow she had got smaller, or Hugo and Smiffy had got bigger, and she could fit comfortably without bursting the cardboard walls.

'Hi, Emily,' Ruth said happily. 'Isn't this lovely?'

'Ruth . . . Oh my g— It worked! The spell worked!'

'It certainly looks that way. I went through the whole rigmarole before I went to sleep, and the next thing I knew, I was here!'

Emily moved closer to the screen, wishing she

could dive into it and join Ruth inside the picture. Now that the camera had pulled back to show the whole room, she could see a large window looking out on a beautiful garden.

And beyond that garden – Bluey? Holly?

'I haven't been outside yet,' said Ruth. 'The magic – or whatever – won't let me. Every time I try to go out, I end up back here. But I'm having a lovely time – Smiffy picked me some fresh marshmallows from the marshmallow tree.'

She broke off and coughed loudly.

'Have some Bearcorf,' said Smiffy. He opened a cupboard, took out a blue bottle and put it on the table. 'I know you're not a bear, but it might work on a human.'

'Bearcorf? Good grief – another of my inventions!' Ruth was chuckling now. 'I invented it when Danny was seven and he had a bad cough. Smiffy had to have a cough too, to keep him company – even though toys don't get coughs. Danny hated the taste of his medicine, so he decided that Smiffy's medicine had to be the most delicious thing in the world: a wondrous compound of chocolate, golden syrup, candyfloss – all his favourite flavours.'

She coughed again, and Emily felt a stab of uneasiness.

'Ruth, where are you – really?'

'I'm in Hugo and Smiffy's kitchen,' Ruth said happily – and rather breathlessly. She patted Smiffy's head. 'It's gorgeous here, Emily. And next time you can come too!'

'I mean ... where's your body? Are you asleep at home?'

'Shhh!' said Ruth. 'We mustn't forget we're on TV.'

Hugo took a step closer to the camera. 'Ruth is a human from the hard world,' he solemnly told his television audience. 'I don't know how she got into our house.'

'Hey, Hugo!' a shrill voice called out. 'It's ten past four!'

The voice came from a large cuckoo clock on the wall. Emily's granny had a cuckoo clock and she knew that the cuckoo was supposed to pop out through a pair of little doors, calling out the hour in musical tones. This cuckoo only put his little wooden head through the doors, and he wasn't bothering to sound musical.

'Ten past! You're late again,' Hugo said crossly. 'Where have you been?'

'Stuck in traffic. It's the rush hour.' The cuckoo disappeared, slamming the little doors behind him.

'I'm going to fire that useless bird!' fumed Hugo. 'I told him, four EXACTLY!'

'At least he came himself this time,' said Smiffy. 'I don't like it when he sends his friends to do it instead. A completely strange plastic lizard popped out last week, and I was so shocked that I dropped my trifle.'

'Quick, I'll sweep the floor – you tidy up those colouring books and crayons.' The fusspot penguin suddenly had a broom. 'Our German lodger is awake – you know he always wakes up for his tea!'

'He's very important,' Smiffy explained to Ruth. 'We don't know exactly what he does because it's a secret. Although truthfully, he spends most of his time sleeping.'

Hugo and Smiffy hurried to finish the last bit of tidying.

Emily had wondered about the German lodger, and was fascinated to see, in a corner of the screen, an ancient bear coming slowly down the stairs.

And a moment later he was in the kitchen – a tall bear with a long snout and reddish-brown fur. He was in perfect condition, not a stitch missing, but Emily quickly saw that he was very old indeed. His fur was patchy and faded.

The German lodger yawned and said, 'Good evening.'

Hugo and Smiffy said, 'Good evening.'

'I will have supper in my room – a small boiled dark-chocolate Easter egg, with two thin slices of toasted fudge cake.' Suddenly and disconcertingly, the German lodger looked directly into the camera. 'And tell Ruth her house is on fire.'

Eleven

FIRE

THE SCREEN WENT BLANK, the sitting room plunged into shadowy darkness.

'Ruth!' Emily jumped up, and for a hideous sick moment she didn't know what to do first. Wake up Mum and Dad? No, there wasn't time, not if this was really happening – but was it really happening? She was barefoot, but her slippers and all her shoes were upstairs. She dashed out of the house into the dark street, moaning and ouching to herself at the coldness and lumpiness of the ground.

She had expected to see flames shooting out of Barkstone Bygones – but everything in the street was quiet and still.

Emily peered into the window of the shop, which looked completely normal.

It wasn't real. I listened to a bear from an imagined land.

The relief was huge. She could even smile at herself for being such an idiot.

Just to make sure, she went round to Ruth's back door and looked through the letterbox.

And at that very moment, the smoke alarm began to beep upstairs.

'RUTH!' Emily hammered at the door, shouting as loud as she could. 'RUTH – WAKE UP – FIRE! RUTH!'

She dashed back home to call the fire brigade and wake her parents. Two huge fire engines and an ambulance arrived a few minutes later. It was like one of Holly's emergencies, with flashing lights in the street, except that this time the drama was happening next door.

They found a small fire spitting inside Ruth's upstairs boiler cupboard, which had made the whole house hazy with smoke.

Ruth was unconscious from inhaling the smoke, but she woke up while she was being carried downstairs by two firefighters in one of her kitchen chairs. She was foggy and befuddled, and amazed to find herself sitting on the pavement outside her shop.

She coughed for a few minutes and took great gulps of the cold night air.

'Are you OK?' Emily knelt down on the pavement beside her.

Ruth croaked, 'The German lodger!'

'What was that?' Emily's mother asked. 'Something about Podge? Don't worry about him, he's sulking behind our shed.' Mum was good at emergencies. She had draped a blanket over Ruth's shoulders and brought her a mug of sweet tea. 'Just carry on taking big breaths of fresh air. I can't get over how lucky you've been – if Emily hadn't been awake to hear your smoke alarm . . .'

'Thanks, Emily,' said Ruth. 'I believe you've just saved my life.' She pulled her closer and whispered, 'It wasn't the boiler – we can't ever do this again!'

They were surrounded by firefighters and paramedics (and the Barkstone police car and several neighbours with trays of tea) and she couldn't say more; though Emily's tongue positively itched with questions, she knew she would have to wait until Ruth managed to catch her on her own.

★

133

Ruth tapped on the glass pane in the back door the next afternoon, while Emily was doing her homework in the kitchen.

'Are your parents around?'

'Mum's gone shopping in London,' Emily said. 'And Dad's doing something in the garage.'

'Good.'

'How are you?'

'Totally fine – especially now I know the insurance will cover my boiler.' Ruth was carrying a large flowerpot, overflowing with greenery. She put it on the kitchen table and it filled the room with the fresh scent of outside. 'This is a small thank-you present for last night. It's the mini herb garden I started to make for Holly.'

'I remember,' Emily said. 'The indoor smelling garden.'

'That's it – everything has a smell. There's lemon thyme, basil, rosemary, mint.' Ruth picked off a mint leaf, crushed it between her fingers and held it out under Emily's nose, giving her a whiff of toothpaste. 'I carried on with it after she died and it looked so pretty in my greenhouse this morning that I thought I'd give it to you. I'll help

134

you with the upkeep. I suggest you put it here on the windowsill.'

The leaves were of every shape – round, spiked, oval – and every shade of green. Ruth was a famously good gardener, and she had often brought in leaves and flowers for Holly to sniff. Her smelling garden was beautifully set out, like a miniature enchanted forest.

Big enough for Bluey to get lost in.

'It's lovely,' Emily said. 'But you don't have to thank me for anything.'

'You listened to the German lodger. Some people would've dismissed it all as a dream and gone back to bed. If you'd done that last night, I'd have died and my shop would have burned to the ground.'

This was a sickening thought. 'Is the shop OK?'

'Fine – I'm only shut today because of the smoky smell upstairs.'

'It's odd that the smoke alarm didn't start until just after I got there,' Emily said. 'I had to tell a few lies to explain how I just happened to be there when your boiler went wrong.'

'We both know it wasn't a coincidence.' Ruth was very serious. 'It was all because of that wretched spell.'

'Did the spell start the fire?'

'I don't know. But this morning I remembered one of the books I collected for research. It used to be a children's classic, though nobody's read it for years – *At the Back of the North Wind*. It's a Victorian story about a little boy who visits a magical land behind the North Wind. The point is that he can only go back to that land when he dies.'

'But . . . you visited The Sycamores in your dreams, and you didn't die.'

'Think about it,' Ruth said. 'I wasn't dreaming, was I? When you saw me on television, my real body was already unconscious from the smoke. I was still alive, and that's why I couldn't get out of the toys' kitchen to explore Deep Smockeroon.'

'But if you'd died—'

'Exactly! Just like the land at the back of the North Wind, it's a place you can only get to if you're dead.'

They were both quiet for a moment, thinking about this.

Emily said, 'Like . . . heaven.'

'I was enormously happy,' Ruth said softly. 'And I felt somehow that Danny was very close. So it does sound rather heavenly.'

'Were you sorry to come back?'

'Was I sorry?' Ruth was startled. 'Yes – for the first few seconds I was very sad to find myself back in real life.'

Emily's mouth was dry; her next question was so daring that she could hardly shape the words. 'When your son died, did you ever wish you could die too?'

'Hmm.' Ruth narrowed her eyes thoughtfully. 'You have to swear never to repeat this to anyone.'

'I swear!'

'The honest answer is . . . yes. I was very afraid of death, but at the same time I wanted to die just to end the pain.'

Emily understood about the pain, which was so much worse than any sort of physical pain. She knew that she didn't want to die herself – but would it be different if she knew for certain that she would see Holly again?

There were voices outside on the front path; a moment later the front door slammed and Emily's mum breezed into the kitchen.

'Ruth!' Mum bent to kiss her cheek. 'How are you?' She was laden with glossy carrier bags and smiling dreamily. 'I've done some wonderful shopping – Em, I know your friend Martha wants a book token for her birthday, but I couldn't resist buying a little present for Pippa.'

'What?' Emily shot a look of alarm at Ruth.

'I'm sure these will fit her.' With a satisfied air, Mum produced a plastic box of tiny frocks for teddy bears. 'The orange one will look nice with her yellow fur.'

'Mum! She's going to be twelve – not four!'

'Yes, but you told me how much Pippa means to her.'

'No I didn't!'

Mum ignored this – or possibly didn't hear it. But Emily was absolutely certain that she had never told her about Martha's yellow bear.

Had Mum been seeing things from Smockeroon, too?

Twelve

AN OLD FRIEND IN
A STRANGE PLACE

'LAST NIGHT I HAD my craziest dream ever,' said
Martha. 'I actually woke up laughing.'

Emily didn't know how it had happened, but she
was well and truly part of Martha's lunch group;
today Amber Frost had even saved a place for her. It
felt very good to be part of a group, and to have people
who wanted to be her friend. The only drawback was
that there was less time for writing in the Bluey book,
just when there was so much to report.

'I love your dreams,' said Amber Jones. 'What was
it about this time – that bear again?'

'Her name is Pippa,' Martha said, pretending to
be strict. 'Don't just call her "that bear". You'll hurt
her feelings.'

They all giggled at this.

'So what was the dream?' Emily tried to sound casual and not burning with curiosity; what was going on? Her mother was buying little frocks for teddy bears, and this was the third time Martha had dreamed about Smockeroon. The magic was spreading.

'I wasn't at a tea party this time,' said Martha. 'I was in a lovely sort of park with very bright colours. And Pippa was there – wearing a sweet little hat – telling me something about a factory where she worked.'

(Seam-Rite!)

Amber Frost asked, 'Like Norton's?'

'No, much nicer. More like a garden than a factory. There was a brass band, and lots of toys dancing.' Martha frowned suddenly. 'And I've just remembered something else. This doll barged in – a really dirty rag doll, with a mad face and plaits made of red knitting wool – and she yelled something about her right to be something or other— Emily? Are you OK?'

Emily had gasped aloud and now pretended to be coughing.

It couldn't be!

Here was another sign – partly thrilling and partly creepy – that the imaginary world was leaking into the

140

real one, and the only person she could talk to was Ruth. It was Monday, not one of her afternoons at the shop, but Emily was sure she could find an excuse to run next door. She spent the rest of the school day simmering with impatience, and so distracted that Mrs Lewis had to shout at her twice before her attention was dragged back to reality.

And then the journey home was maddeningly slow because the lashing rain had brought the traffic to a standstill.

'Ugh, this weather!' Mum peered anxiously through the spaces made by the windscreen wipers (the regular swish-swish-swish was like Holly's breathing machine). 'That meadow will be a sea of mud by now. It's a good thing they finished before it started.'

'Hmm – sorry?'

'You're miles away! I was telling you about the burnt tree – the workmen appeared in the wildlife meadow this morning and dug up the whole thing, roots and all.'

'Oh.'

'It looks a mess, and horribly empty. I miss that lovely tree. They'll plant something else, of course; it won't always be like the Somme.'

There was a queue of cars waiting at the roundabout. They slowed to a crawl and the rain came down in torrents.

'Oh, this rain!' Mum suddenly chuckled, and added, 'This pibbly-pobbly rain!'

When Emily was four, Bluey had made up a song –

> *The rain! The rain!*
> *The pibbly-pobbly rain!*
> *It's such a nasty day*
> *We can't go out to play!*

This was the first time Mum had referred to Bluey and his world since Holly died. Emily caught her breath, waiting for the memory to shatter into sadness, but her mother went on smiling.

'You were such a funny little thing – always making up songs and stories. Do you remember when Dad accidentally said the rain was "pibbly-pobbly" to his boss?' They both laughed, and Mum was still cheerful when they got home.

'Ruth's shut today; the new boiler's being fitted and I don't know if her heating's back yet – would you be an angel and check that she's all right?'

'OK.' This was the perfect opportunity to bring Ruth up to speed. Emily hurried out of the car and through the downpour, and started gabbling about Martha's dream as soon as Ruth opened her back door.

'Slow down – take a breath and count to ten.' Ruth firmly pushed her into the kitchen and made her sit down at the table. 'So your friend had a dream about a dirty rag doll?'

'Yes, and I think I know that doll in the hard world!'

'Good grief,' said Ruth. 'Is she one of yours?'

'No – she used to belong to Maze when we were at nursery school. I suddenly remembered her when Martha described her mad face and red wool plaits. Her name's Prison Wendy.'

'It's what?'

'Prizzy for short. She was very naughty and always being sent to prison.'

Ruth snorted with laughter. 'But toys don't have prisons!'

'It wasn't a toys' prison.' Emily hadn't thought about Maze's dirty rag doll for years, and now the memories were rushing back. 'It was an old shoebox on the top shelf. Maze's mother used to put Prison Wendy in the box when our games with her got too rowdy – when Maze made her climb up the chimney or spill the painting water. I think she must've been quite a posh rag doll once. But then she got so sooty and smelly that they put her in the washing machine and her face wore off. So Maze drew her a new face with a mad wonky smile.'

'Poor old Prison Wendy!' Ruth was still chuckling. 'Do you know where she is now?'

'No,' Emily said. 'I know she's not in Maze's bedroom. I haven't seen her since I was little.' How come Martha was seeing toys from Smockeroon? She thought she'd been dreaming, with no idea that she was seeing a real place.

I must find a way to tell her.

A sudden movement under the table made them both jump.

Hugo's voice floated up at them. '. . . one barrel of Tudbury's Drinking Syrup, and two boxes of plain chocolate eggs. And please deliver it to The Sycamores.'

Emily bent down and saw Daniel's cardboard box, with the furry head of the penguin sticking out of the flap. 'Hi, Hugo.' She pulled the box out into the middle of the floor. 'What are you doing here?'

It was very funny to see Hugo's frown of annoyance.

'Not again! Can't a penguin pop out to the sweet shop without being whisked off Hardside?' He was wearing a hat made of purple velvet, in the shape of a saucepan – the gold-painted handle stuck out jauntily on one side.

Emily lifted him out of the box and put him on the table. 'Was it the broken door again?'

'I don't know what it was – I thought I was in Pointed End!'

The cardboard box on the floor trembled and out popped the head of Smiffy, wearing an orange velvet-covered saucepan with a silver handle.

'Let me guess,' said Ruth. 'The saucepan hats are Pointed End's latest fashion statement?'

'Hello, Ruth,' said Smiffy. 'Yes, that's right. Don't they look stylish?'

Both toys looked so proud that Ruth and Emily quickly said, 'Yes – very stylish,' and did their best not to laugh.

'I've come to fetch Hugo,' Smiffy said. 'It's time to make the German lodger's tea – the cuckoo in the clock sent me a text.'

'A text!' snapped Hugo. 'Of all the cheek! He's

just taking advantage because we can't tell the time ourselves – I've a good mind to complain to the Sturvey!'

Emily asked, 'Has the Sturvey replied to your message yet?'

'No,' said Smiffy. 'It's very strange. Normally he gets right back to you.'

So the Sturvey is a 'he'; does that mean he's a toy?

'Does he call you back? Do you speak to him?'

Hugo and Smiffy looked puzzled.

'Nobody speaks to the Sturvey,' said Hugo. 'Normally, when you leave a message, things just get put right.'

'But things aren't being put right at the moment,' said Smiffy. 'We're not the only toys being kept waiting. The stuffed hippos next door asked for a playground extension weeks ago, and nothing's happened yet.'

'Maybe he – or it – is extra busy at the moment,' said Ruth.

'We'll keep on trying,' said Hugo. 'Come on, Smiffy – we'd better make the German lodger's tea.'

He suddenly scuttled across the table and took a headlong dive into the cardboard box. Smiffy shouted, 'Wait for me!' – there was a flash of light and the box closed on two ordinary stuffed toys.

Emily was disappointed. 'I thought Hugo was going to explain more about the Sturvey!'

'No he wasn't,' Ruth said. 'He bolted back to Smockeroon because he has no idea who the Sturvey is and he's too vain to admit it – I know that penguin, don't forget.' She had stopped smiling. 'I wish I knew exactly why this is happening to us. I wonder if it's my fault.'

'What do you mean?'

Ruth said, 'I didn't put Hugo and Smiffy in Danny's coffin. When it came to the point, I just couldn't bring myself to do it – I couldn't bear to lose them too. But I worried about it afterwards.' Tears trembled in her eyes. 'I worried that he was lonely without them.'

'He's not lonely.' Emily put her small, nail-bitten hand on top of Ruth's plump one. 'Hugo and Smiffy said they see him all the time.'

The cat flap in the kitchen door sprang open, and Podge poured through it with an angry yowl.

'What's up, old boy?' Ruth bent down to stroke his striped head. 'Have those squirrels been bothering you?'

The cat flap opened again. For one second Emily thought some wild animal was coming after the cowardly old pet. But the muddy creature that climbed through the flap was smaller than a squirrel, and it had four little wheels and a tail.

It spoke in a voice like rough sandpaper. 'Come on, you two – it's nice and warm in here.'

Thirteen

THE NEW LODGERS

EVEN IF YOU WERE USED to toys moving and talking, it was a very weird sight. Emily and Ruth stared, transfixed, as two more muddy toys clambered through the cat flap. The one with the sandpaper voice was a wooden donkey on wheels and he had been joined by a clanky metallic monkey and a small grubby bear.

The three little figures carefully wiped their feet (or wheels) on the doormat.

'Good grief!' whispered Ruth. 'It's them!'

'Sorry?' Emily didn't understand why Ruth was so excited. 'Who?'

Ruth made a dive at one of the piles of books on the table and pulled out the biography of John Staples. 'Don't you recognise them?' She opened it at the black-and-white photograph of the three toys that had belonged to the Staples children – Blokey the tin monkey, Mokey the wooden donkey and Figinda Faraway, the small plush bear.

'Of course!' Emily knelt down to look at the famous Edwardian toys more closely. They were nothing like modern toys, which were mostly either soft and cuddly or battery-operated. Under the dirt, these three antiques were small and wizened, with odd little faces that were vivid with personality. 'But where did they come from?'

'That was a very long walk,' the monkey said (in a voice that creaked and scraped like a rusty hinge). 'Humans' doormats are extremely prickly! Now, who's in charge of this cafe?'

The donkey raised his head to look at Ruth and Emily. 'The old fat one, I should think.'

'Can you hear me, fat old lady?' called the monkey. 'We'd like three mugs of Biggins' Mixture. Any flavour except lemon-and-lime.'

'Fat old lady!' Ruth burst out laughing. 'Look, I'm sorry, I think you must've made a mistake – this isn't a cafe.'

'You're not in Smockeroon,' Emily said, as kindly as she could. 'This is the hard world.'

'Oh, we know that,' the donkey said cheerfully.

'We were blown back here all of a sudden, when the diggers uncovered our trunk this morning.'

'Diggers?'

'Don't you see?' Ruth was half excited and half laughing. 'Where else would John have buried them? They were under the tree – and when the tree surgeons ripped out the roots—'

'But that doesn't explain what they're doing here.' Emily carefully picked up the three toys and put them on the table. They were very light and she shivered to feel them wriggling in her fingers. 'Why aren't they just dumb toys?'

'I think the rules must've changed,' said Figinda Faraway. 'It was rather peculiar.'

'We were in our house, in the very deepest part of Smockeroon,' said Blokey the monkey. 'So deep that nobody can leave – when things are normal, anyway. All of a sudden there was a flash of white light, and then I found myself holding a Hardside permit from the Sturvey. We sent the request more than fifty years ago and it got turned down because we were in too deep. But the law must've changed.'

'We can't ask him about it,' said Mokey the donkey. 'Nobody's seen him for ages.'

'Have you ever seen him?' Emily asked eagerly.

'Oh, yes,' said Blokey, nodding his little tin head. 'He lived next door to us at one time. But he has a very important government job, and that keeps him very busy.'

'Is he a toy?'

'He's a bear,' said Figinda Faraway solemnly. 'The most imagined bear in all the world, packed with imagination! And he has very elegant manners.'

So the Sturvey was not a government building, nor was he a wizard. He was just an old bear, according to these toys.

'John said we could come,' Mokey put in creakily. 'If we promised to be good.'

'John Staples?' Ruth was pale with mingled amazement and fear. 'Good grief!'

Emily knew why she was scared. It was one thing to meet modern, living toys like Hugo and Smiffy and Notty – but these three toys had come from the land of the dead. 'How did you get here?'

'That was the diggers,' said the tin monkey. 'Everything suddenly went dark and cold, and I was the first to realise that we'd somehow come back into the hard world, where we haven't been for years. And

I said to the others, "Mark my words, we're back in the trunk!"'

'In the trunk where he put us,' said Mokey. 'To save us from being burned.'

Ruth asked, 'Did you try to go back to Smockeroon – or are you trapped here?'

The three old toys looked puzzled.

'Trapped? Good gracious, no!' Figinda Faraway said briskly. 'Naturally we went straight back to Smockeroon, but we couldn't get to our bit.'

'You've lost me,' said Ruth. 'Your bit?'

'My dear fat lady, try to keep up! We live in the very deepest part of Smockeroon, which is sometimes called the Land of Neverendings, and sometimes the Enchanted Forest. It's where all the imagination goes.'

And the dead people.

Holly and Danny.

It was unbearably exciting to think that these toys had come from that mysterious region – where Christopher Robin still played with Winnie-the-Pooh, though the real Christopher Robin had died an old man and the real Pooh lived in a glass case in New York.

'And when we tried to go home,' Figinda Faraway

went on, 'we were in a different part of Smockeroon. The modern part, where all the toys can come and go from the Hardside because their owners are still alive. It's a very attractive place, once you get used to the noise.'

'We've decided to stay at a boarding house we saw in the newspaper,' Blokey said cheerfully. 'It's called The Sycamores. I'll send them a telegram to say we've arrived.'

'You're a bit behind the times,' said Ruth. 'Telegrams don't exist nowadays. It's all mobile phones, even in Smockeroon.'

'I've seen Hugo with a phone,' Emily said, 'but we don't know his number.'

'Hang on, we don't need his number – he's right here!' Ruth leaned down to Daniel's box and triumphantly pulled out Hugo and Smiffy. 'Wake up, boys! Your new lodgers have just turned up in my . . .'

Her voice trailed away as she realised she was talking to a pair of soft toys.

'Why can't we summon them?' Emily reached out to stroke Hugo. 'Aren't they supposed to come when we call them?'

'I expect they're too busy,' Figinda Faraway piped

up. 'Their bodies are here – and that's normally enough for humans. I mean, normally you don't expect them to talk, do you?'

'Well – no . . .'

'The modern part of Smockeroon is simply thrilling! I can't wait to look around – but we had to come to the hard world first. Look at the state of us!' She held up the ragged remnants of what had once been a flowered dress and was now falling apart in her paws like a filthy cobweb. 'We can't go into refined society like this!'

'You see,' said Blokey, 'in the modern part of Smockeroon, toys look the same as they do in the hard world. And in the hard world I find that I'm covered with rust.'

'My paint's wearing off,' said Mokey.

'Oh, I get it,' Emily said. 'You came here because you want us to clean you.'

'That's right,' said Blokey, with a smile on his painted face. 'There was just enough light in our trunk to see how shabby and dirty we are.'

'John buried us in the garden,' said Figinda Faraway. 'He gave us each a kiss and said he'd see us in Smockeroon.'

'And ... did he?' Emily had a sudden stab of longing for Bluey and Holly. 'Did he come to see you?'

'Yes, of course,' said Blokey. 'He knew we'd never leave him.'

'And every visit drove us in deeper,' said Figinda Faraway – as if this explained everything. 'More than a hundred Hard years have passed, so it's not our fault we're so filthy. And the long walk through all that mud made it worse.'

'We can get some of the mud off, at least.' Ruth produced a packet of new J-cloths. She ran them under the hot tap and gave one to Emily, and they carefully cleaned the top layer of mud off the three old toys – it was funny to see the donkey screwing up his painted face while Ruth dabbed at him.

'I need a new dress,' said Figinda Faraway. 'Smart but not too formal.'

Emily suddenly remembered the packet of little dresses that Mum had bought for Martha's bear Pippa. 'Back in a minute!'

She ran to her house, where her mother was doing some paperwork for her job at the kitchen table, and did not notice when Emily quickly took the little dresses out of the drawer.

'I was just about to call you – supper's nearly ready.'

Emily gabbled a quick lie about borrowing the dustpan and brush, and pelted back next door.

'Emily, you're a genius!' said Ruth, beaming. 'Look, Figinda – six new dresses!'

The small white bear stared at the six new dresses. For a moment Emily was afraid she didn't like them – but the grubby furry face stretched into a radiant smile.

'Oh, they're lovely – thank you, Emily! Could I try on the pink one?'

Ruth gently removed Figinda's rags and helped her into the pink dress. It fitted perfectly. Emily brought the small mirror from the downstairs toilet and the antique toy admired herself from all angles. (Ruth and Emily had to struggle not to laugh; the little bear looked very funny but they didn't want to hurt her feelings.) 'You've both been most kind,' said Mokey. 'Now we'd like to go back to modern Smockeroon and check in to The Sycamores. I booked by public telephone and spoke to a penguin.'

'I'm terribly sorry, but that might not be possible—' began Ruth.

'Hurry up, Smiffy!' cried a bossy voice under the table. 'Our new lodgers have arrived.'

The cardboard box quivered and out jumped Hugo, closely followed by Smiffy – and a cloud of blue glitter when Smiffy dropped a big tray of toys' cakes on the kitchen floor.

The three Staples toys went to the edge of the table; when he saw them, the penguin bowed deeply. 'Welcome!'

'So you're in charge of The Sycamores,' said Blokey. 'How do you do. We'd all love a mug of Biggins' Mixture.'

'It's so nice to hear them talking about Biggins'!' Ruth burst out happily. 'It's a hot drink for very old toys that are stuffed with sawdust – Danny invented it when we visited a toy museum.'

'Notty's stuffed with sawdust,' Emily said. 'Maybe he has some.'

'I'll ask him,' said Smiffy. 'Or Bluey.'

'Bluey!' Emily's heart skipped. 'He's not— I mean, he wasn't stuffed with sawdust!'

'No, but he lives next door to a really old rabbit,' Smiffy explained (with a kind expression on his sweet and foolish face that pierced Emily with sudden longing for Bluey and his owner).

'We should be going,' said Blokey. 'It's nearly seven o'clock.'

Hugo and Smiffy gaped at him in amazement.

'Wow,' whispered Hugo. 'You can tell the time!'

The tin monkey looked rather smug. 'Naturally.'

'Now we can fire that lazy cuckoo,' said Smiffy happily. 'Come along, everyone!'

He opened the cardboard box, letting out a glow of white light. All the toys jumped into the box (Mokey did a showy dive off the table, shouting, 'Wheee!') and it closed behind them.

Ruth and Emily were left dazed and blinking in a kitchen that had returned to the solid drabness of the hard world. Ruth opened Daniel's box and they both stared in silence at the heap of dumb toys inside it.

'I've just thought of something,' Ruth said, stroking Figgy's new dress. 'These toys are not my property. They belong to the Staples estate – in money terms, they must be worth a small fortune. Maybe I should hand them in at the police station.'

'Not yet!' Emily begged. 'Can't we just hold on to them for a while?' Though she couldn't put it into words, the Edwardian toys gave her a sense of nearness to Bluey. 'They might be able to help us find out how the magic is leaking out of Smockeroon.'

'Never mind what's getting out,' Ruth said. 'It's what's getting *in* to Smockeroon that bothers me. I can't bear to think of that happy place being invaded by sadness.'

Fourteen

IT BEGINS

THE NEXT MORNING they were giving Maze a lift to school.

In the old days she would have run down their gardens to the back door. Today, however, she knocked on the front door, like a stranger.

'Hi, Maze!' Dad was just setting off to the pie factory on his bicycle. 'Nice to see you!'

'Hello, Maze – you're bang on time!' Mum beamed at her. 'It's been ages, hasn't it?'

Maze's cheeks were red and the thunderous look in her dark eyes made Emily's stomach turn nervous somersaults. For some reason – though Mum and Dad didn't notice a thing – Maze was furious. Instead of the usual torrent of talking, she was ominously quiet.

Emily had no idea what she was supposed to have

done. When her mother's back was turned, she mouthed, 'What?'

Maze only scowled at her and spent most of the journey across town in glowering silence. When the car stopped outside the gates of Hatty Catty, she mumbled, 'Thanks,' and got out so fast that Emily practically had to chase her through the main doors.

'Maze – wait! What is it? What've I done?'

Maze hissed, 'Like you don't know!'

'But I don't!'

They were on the big staircase that led up to the classrooms, and because they were quite early it was deserted.

'You think it's funny, don't you?' Maze suddenly whisked round and grabbed Emily's arm. 'You and that pathetic Martha Bishop!'

'Ow – that really hurts!' Emily tried to tug her arm away. 'Look, could you please just tell me?'

A door opened on the landing above them. 'You two Year Sevens – stop that messing about!'

It was Mrs Lewis, glaring down at them like a cross, white-haired gargoyle. Maze stopped pinching Emily's arm.

A big gaggle of Year Nine girls came charging past

them up the stairs, all chattering at the tops of their voices, and Mrs Lewis was distracted.

'So you don't know anything about THIS!' Maze was holding a tatty scrap of paper, which she shoved at Emily. 'You put it in my pocket!'

One side of the paper was covered with crude writing in what looked like purple wax crayon – HAHAHA YoU aRE a BUM!!!!

Emily drew in a sharp breath. This note had not been written by a human. Suddenly she knew exactly who had sent it, and blurted it out before she knew what she was doing.

'Maze, this isn't from me – it's from Prizzy! Don't you remember her insulting messages?'

The name of the old rag doll hit Maze like a slap. 'Don't be stupid – I know what this is! You're using our babyish old game to make me feel guilty – because I don't give poor little boohoo Emily enough attention!'

'You ... what?' The injustice was breathtaking.

'I've got new friends now.' Maze drew a couple of breaths and hurriedly added, 'Look, I'm sorry, OK?' Her angry face flushed a deeper red and she dashed away up the stairs.

Emily was left stunned, clutching the rude note that was obviously the work of Prison Wendy. Maze had said 'sorry', but not as if she meant it.

I've been well and truly DUMPED.

Before she could think about it properly, Martha and Amber Jones came running up the stairs.

'Hi, Emily,' Martha said breathlessly. 'My uncle Mike – the one who bought the beer I won in the raffle – he's in the fire brigade and he told me about the fire in your friend's shop. He says you're a heroine. Why didn't you tell us?'

'Oh, I didn't really do anything . . .'

'Mike said the lady could have died from inhaling the smoke long before anyone noticed the flames. I hope she's OK.'

'Yes, she's—'

'Mike's the uncle who did the nude calendar for charity – he's Mr August. My other uncle's a vicar. He says he'd love to be in a nude calendar but nobody's asked him.'

Thanks to Martha, Emily was laughing when she walked into the classroom – and the pain of seeing Maze muttering to Summer wasn't nearly as bad as she thought it would be. She wasn't sitting alone at her desk any more. She had a circle of really nice friends.

Martha tugged at her sleeve and whispered, 'Look, hope you don't mind, I haven't asked Maze and Summer to my party. I don't think they would have wanted to come, anyway.'

'That's fine by me,' said Emily, suddenly remembering the sleepover. 'It's your birthday.'

She thought of her own birthday, at the end of February. She had never had big parties because of Holly. When Holly was alive, they had celebrated Emily's birthday with a small tea party and Maze had been the only guest – a great guest, who sang songs and made Holly smile.

How could she forget?

Does she even care that Holly died?

★

Emily's parents had joined a club called The Barkstone Bookworms. They met once a fortnight in someone's sitting room, and spent the evening drinking wine and talking about a book they had all read. This evening, eight Bookworms – including

Ruth – had gathered at Emily's house. Judging by the loud voices and roars of laughter behind the sitting-room door, it wasn't a very serious discussion.

Emily sat at the kitchen table with the laptop, watching a documentary about penguins in the Antarctic. Real penguins who were not toys had a terrible time – lashed by snowstorms, waddling for miles to find food. Hugo would have hated it.

She couldn't stop thinking about John's spell, and the sudden appearance of his three toys. Ruth had put Blokey, Mokey and Figinda in Daniel's box, and she managed to whisper to Emily that she hadn't heard a squeak out of them.

But something has changed.

Ruth had left the rest of their 'potion' in a plastic bottle on the shelf in her kitchen, and Emily was sure she'd forgotten all about it – her kitchen was packed with old bottles and jars.

What if that fire had nothing to do with the spell?

The Staples brothers had used the spell to visit Smockeroon every night, and they hadn't died.

I bet one more try wouldn't hurt.

It was very frustrating to know that she might be just one short step away from Holly, if only she could persuade Ruth to change her mind about trying the spell again.

Dad hurried in to the kitchen to fetch more wine and beer from the fridge. 'You OK, Em?'

'I'm fine.'

'Sorry about the noise – we just voted to read a new book. We were all sick of *The Great Gatsby* so now we've changed it to *Winnie-the-Pooh*.'

Lord Pooh and Lord Piglet.

Emily quickly wrote this down in the Bluey book after Dad had gone back to the Bookworms; she'd forgotten that in her stories for Holly these famous characters and several other well-known toys (Dogger, Bagpuss) were lords and ladies in Smockeroon. And then she wondered about the oddness of it. Only yesterday Dad had been calling *The Great* whatsit the masterpiece of the twentieth century. Now he was reading *Winnie-the-Pooh*. It didn't make sense – unless this was a sign that the magic was seeping out into the hard world in a very serious way.

'... and in other news, the terrible jelly flood at Pointed End was caused by a disgruntled wooden cuckoo ...'

She blinked and gasped as a surge of dazzling lights

suddenly came streaming out of the laptop, painting the whole kitchen with the colours of Christmas.

A jelly flood at Pointed End?

As usual, she had to wait for her eyes to adjust to the glare of toys' television. The screen was filled with the solemn face of the lady panda reading the news.

'... claimed that he'd been unfairly fired from his job. Several small toys are still trapped in jelly.'

A series of photos appeared of the gardens around The Sycamores covered in a thick layer of red jelly. And then the screen was filled with a police mugshot of the cuckoo, his wooden features carved into a scowl, and numbers across his chest.

But this isn't right!

Toys were never mean or nasty; it was one of the great rules of Smockeroon. Humans could be mean to each other, but toys were always kind.

The sadness is taking over in Smockeroon.

The panda's face came back. 'And now the weather; don't forget the nine-minute shower of rain due at eighteen past eleven tomorrow morning.'

Some adverts came next and Emily watched them anxiously, looking for more signs of human horridness. It was reassuring to see that everything else in Smockeroon looked as sweet and silly as ever.

I was a bear with terrible CORF,
I corfed so hard my ears blew ORF . . .

She leaned close to the screen, trying to look at the background; those lovely woods and fields of Deep Smockeroon, where Bluey played with Holly, and Hugo and Smiffy played with Danny.

Bluey, where are you?

The announcer's voice said, 'And now a brand-new series – *My Owner's Bedroom*.'

There was a burst of music; the screen filled with a view of a human bedroom, quite a lot like Emily's own bedroom. A human was sitting at the desk – a girl with curly brown hair and a sweet, dimpled face.

It was Martha Bishop, and she didn't seem to have a clue that she was on television.

'Martha?'

But Martha obviously couldn't hear her; she carried on eating crisps and reading her book.

'Hello. I'm Pippa. Welcome to *My Owner's Bedroom*!'

Yes, it was Pippa, the little yellow Seam-Rite bear,

beaming with pride as she showed off Martha's stuff. Why didn't she notice?

'Finally, my favourite thing,' said Pippa, pulling open a drawer. 'This wonderful five-pack of new knickers!'

Emily burst out laughing – much as she yearned to see Bluey, she was glad he didn't discuss her knickers on TV. Embarrassing! Even if it was only seen by a bunch of toys.

'And now for a newsflash.' The panda was back. 'Reports are coming in that the Sturvey's office is broken. Hundreds of toys have complained about not-answered messages and there are fears that the Great Sturvey himself has vanished.'

The sitting-room door opened, the light turned normal again and the penguins were back on the laptop. It was annoying not to hear any more of this incredible story.

What has happened to the Great Sturvey?

The bear had apparently disappeared leaving Smockeroon to slide into chaos.

The Bookworms were roaring with laughter and yelling out a song that contained the word 'tiddely-pom'. They said their goodbyes and left the house with a noise like the pub turning out at closing time.

And they were all such quiet, grey-haired, respectable people.

Though she wasn't exactly scared, Emily had a strong sense that the magic was more out of control than ever.

'What a fascinating discussion that was!' Ruth was staying for a cup of tea. Her face was flushed and her eyes were glazed and dreamy.

Dad said, 'It's a masterpiece of the twentieth century, perhaps the masterpiece. And I think next time I might dress up as Eeyore.'

'Brilliant!' said Mum. 'And we can eat honey and condensed milk, like Pooh.'

Emily's parents both had a weird, other-worldly look to them, and Emily felt a first flutter of alarm; couldn't they hear what they were saying? She tried to catch Ruth's eye, but nobody would look at her properly.

Dad started to chat about his work, and at first he sounded perfectly normal. 'We're pretty busy at the moment, launching a new range of fruit pies.' But then silliness took over again, when he added,

171

'They're special throwing-pies – you know – for pie fights.'

'Marvellous!' said Mum.

'Genius!' said Ruth.

Now Emily was really alarmed. *Get your party going – with a pie that's for THROWING!*

This was more than a small leak. The unique silliness of Smockeroon had seeped into the largest food factory in the West Midlands.

'Ruth!' she hissed.

'Tiddely-pom,' said Ruth.

In desperation, Emily sloshed some of her hot tea (not hot enough to scald) on the back of Ruth's hand.

'Ouch!' Ruth blinked hard for a few minutes, and frowned to herself, as if trying to work out a difficult sum.

And then she looked at Emily properly, and murmured, 'Oh dear.'

Fifteen

THE SERPENT IN
THE GARDEN

THE STRANGEST THING of all was that everything was so normal the next morning. Emily and her parents ate a normal breakfast, Dad cycled off to the factory in a totally normal way, and there was no more ridiculous talk about throwing-pies. (Emily had tested this by asking Dad a casual question about his work, and all he'd said was, 'Oh, it's the same old grind – moving around columns of numbers.')

Her mother hustled her into the car.

'Hurry up, Em! I want to dodge the traffic.' There was nothing dreamy about Mum this morning. She was brisk and matter-of-fact, and only wanted to talk about taking on an extra day at her work. 'Are you sure you don't mind? Ruth was delighted, by the way – she says she'd love to have you for an extra afternoon.'

'It's fine,' Emily said. 'I like going to Ruth's.'

She longed to talk to Ruth about last night: the alarming attack of silliness, and the sensational news that the Sturvey had been declared missing.

'I think you've given her a new lease of life.' Mum drummed her fingers thoughtfully on the steering wheel while they waited at the roundabout. 'I haven't seen her so jolly since . . . well—'

'Since Daniel died,' Emily said.

'Yes.'

'When her heart was broken.'

Mum was startled. 'Did she tell you that?'

'She didn't need to tell me. I just knew.'

'It must be nearly ten years ago – you were a baby. And Holly—' Mum let out the endless, yearning sigh that Emily had got used to. 'He was a nice boy and he was only eighteen.'

'Poor Ruth!'

'I don't see why I shouldn't tell you,' Mum said, after a long pause. 'It was a road accident – he was on a motorbike. Ruth had to identify his body.'

'Oh.' Emily had not known this, and she had to pretend to be staring out of the window so that her mother wouldn't see that she was crying; it was so sad that she could hardly bear it. No wonder Ruth loved remembering all the happy times in Smockeroon.

'Anyway – it's great to see how much you've cheered her up. It reminds me of how she was before.' Mum sighed again, then added, in her normal voice, 'Sorry we're so early. I keep forgetting – it doesn't take me an hour to load up the car any more.'

'That's OK. I like being early.' Emily shook away the last tears. 'I can have a coffee from the machine.'

The coffee machine was one of the best things about Hatty Catty; it felt very cool to stride around with a cup of machine coffee like a sixth-former. There was usually a queue, but this morning she was so early that the only person ahead of her was Martha.

'Hi Emily! I'm so glad you showed up early – my dad parked me here at practically dawn because it's market day and he was taking in some pigs.' Martha took her cup of hot chocolate (much nicer than coffee but not nearly as cool). 'Tell me honestly – do I smell piggy?'

'All I can smell is perfume,' Emily said, laughing. 'You must've sprayed it on with a hose!'

'I might've gone a bit mad with it. But I'm not giving that cow Summer any more excuses to make faces at me and "oink" noises, just because I live on a farm.'

'Morning, girls.' Ms Robinson was walking towards them along the corridor. 'You two are keen – don't we set you enough homework?'

'Oh, isn't this sweet?' Martha reached out to stroke a small brown koala bear attached to the zip of Ms Robinson's backpack.

'Meet Koley the Koala key ring,' Ms Robinson said, smiling and looking very young. 'I hadn't seen him for years, and then he suddenly turned up this morning, completely out of the blue! I thought he might like to watch our rehearsal this afternoon.'

Lenny.

Emily was sure Koley had once belonged to Ms Robinson's little brother.

The door between the worlds is broken – that toy has come from Deep Smockeroon.

★

Emily ran into the antique shop as soon as she got back to Barkstone that afternoon, to tell Ruth the news.

176

'Vanished?' Ruth put down the silver teapot she had been cleaning. 'That's impossible!'

'That's what the newsreader said. The Great Sturvey has vanished and his office isn't working.'

'But how will the place keep going without him?' She frowned thoughtfully. 'I wish I knew what to do about it.'

'Have I missed anything here?'

'Nothing dramatic,' said Ruth. 'Except that I rather wish certain toys would go back to Smockeroon sometimes, instead of hanging about while I'm trying to work.'

'Hello, Emily,' said a frayed old voice.

Notty was sitting on the shelf, and so was someone else: Figinda Faraway, in her new dress, with a big pink bow on each ear. They were drinking mugs of something hot.

'I popped in for a drop of Biggins' Mixture,' said Figinda. 'This elegant bear has a good supply.'

Ruth said, 'That place is leaking magic like a colander.' Her voice dropped to a whisper. 'And quite honestly, these old toys are making me incredibly nervous – it's worse than having mice. It's like being infested with mice who can talk – I mean, imagine

177

if you could hear them calling to each other under the floorboards!'

Emily lowered her voice. 'Have they been here all day?'

'Yes,' said Figinda Faraway. 'It's lovely.'

'Go home, you two,' said Ruth. 'Why won't you go home?'

'It's nicer here,' said Notty. 'Pointed End is too full of fighting.'

This was a strange and worrying thing to hear from a dear old teddy bear – and another sign of the sad, mean, hard world seeping into Smockeroon.

'What is there to fight about?' asked Emily.

'Someone broke into The Sycamores and stole the whole top floor,' said Miss Faraway. 'The crime rate has certainly worsened since my day.'

'It's like the story of Adam and Eve,' said Ruth. 'The serpent has entered the Garden of Eden.'

'I have a friend who's a serpent,' said Figinda Faraway. 'She used to work Hardside as a draught-excluder.'

And then Notty said, 'I'm going down to Smartweed's this afternoon, to buy myself one of those trendy novelty farts.'

'Novelty farts?' Ruth laughed softly. 'That was one of Danny's inventions! Toys could buy themselves farts that sounded like a strain of beautiful music!'

'I'll come with you,' said Figinda Faraway. 'I'm trying to catch up on all the latest fashions – we've been so long in Deepest Smockeroon. What tune are you getting?'

'"Greensleeves",' said Notty.

'I fancy "Twinkle, Twinkle".'

Bluey's fart tune would be 'One Bear Went to Mow'.

'Oh, what bliss this is!' Half laughing and half crying, Ruth wiped her eyes. 'But this isn't right – and somehow, we've got to chase out the bad things that have got into Smockeroon ... before they hurt the people we love.'

Holly and Danny.

It was sickening to think that their happy world might be spoiled.

'There must be something we can do!'

'But what?' Ruth shrugged helplessly. 'Call the police? Write to our MP?'

'We've got to find the Sturvey,' Emily said. 'What if the black toad has hurt him?'

'Hang on,' said Ruth. 'Customer alert!'

179

A young woman was peering into the shop window. Ruth jumped from her chair, took the two toys down from the shelf, briskly covered their stitched mouths with sticky-tape and stashed them under the table.

'I don't want anyone else to hear them,' she muttered to Emily. 'This is the drill I worked out, to be on the safe side.'

'I'd better get home now, anyway,' said Emily.

'Would you mind taking out my rubbish? It's the black bag on the kitchen floor.'

The young woman came into the shop. Emily went to the kitchen and found the rubbish bag on the floor. It was while she was tying up the bag that she saw it – a small plastic bottle half-filled with dirty water.

Our magic potion!

Ruth had said the spell was too dangerous, but would it be worth the risk if Emily could see Bluey again? Or Holly?

Emily pulled out the bottle of potion. It was covered with old tea leaves and the water had turned a sinister brown colour, but she felt a charge of excitement when she hid it at the bottom of her bag.

So what if there was a small risk of death?

Sixteen

PIPPA'S
HOLIDAY

EMILY WENT TO BED as early as she could
without making her parents suspicious. She got
into bed clutching the plastic bottle and stared at it
for a long time, working up the courage to swallow a
spoonful of the dingy-looking water.

It tasted musty and sour – could the magic potion
have gone off, like milk?

She lay down on her back, with her arms by her
side, and whispered the rhyme:

Magic mountains, valleys deep,
Let me see you when I sleep! . . .

It was an enormous let-down, but also a relief to wake up the next morning after a night without a single dream.

What did I do wrong?

She wasn't dead, anyway. The day was cold and bright and her room was flooded with sunlight. The hard world had never looked harder.

'Emily!' her mother called. 'Hurry up, or you won't have time for breakfast!'

'I'm coming!' Her voice was croaky with sleep and she didn't want to move, but she forced herself to swing her legs out of bed. Mum was a bit of a dictator in the mornings; if she didn't hear 'feet on the floor' she was quite capable of bursting into Emily's room and whisking off the duvet.

'Em!'

'I said I'm coming!' The good thing about having a school uniform was that you always knew what to wear. Emily hurriedly dragged on her grey skirt, striped tie and white shirt and brushed the tangles out of her hair.

When she came out of her bedroom, she found her mother on the landing beside the boiler-cupboard, her face buried in something soft and pink.

'Mum?'

She hastily wiped her eyes. 'Sorry. I came up for a clean tea towel, and I suddenly came across this – I'd completely forgotten—'

The soft pink thing was a T-shirt, with 'HOLLY' printed on it above a big red heart. They had bought it two years ago while visiting a safari park.

'It took me by surprise,' Mum said. 'I wasn't prepared.'

Emily folded her arms around her mother, hugging her hard. For a few minutes they clung to each other and Mum cried on Emily's shoulder, as if she had been the child and Emily the adult. This hadn't happened when Holly died.

'Oh, darling!' Mum pulled away from her, scrubbing at her eyes, trying to smile. 'I'm so glad I've got you! If you weren't here . . .'

'Well, I am here,' Emily said. 'I'll never leave you.'

Her mother managed a proper smile and turned back into an adult by giving Emily a quick hug. 'You've cheered us all up since the day you were born – and we never meant to have another baby.'

'I know.' Emily had heard this before, though not since Holly died. She liked hearing it.

'You were our brilliant mistake. I'd been worried that a new baby would take away some of the love that Holly needed – but you brought her more love, not less.'

Mum put the T-shirt back in the boiler cupboard and ran downstairs, and the sad moment was over.

Emily quickly sniffed the T-shirt, in case it still smelt of Holly. Her smell had lingered after she died.

Cake and baby wipes.

There was nothing left of it now; all Emily could smell on the T-shirt was a dusty trace of fabric softener.

Dead people leave their special smell behind.

It's partly nice and partly awful.

And then it fades away and that's worse.

The spell had to work before she lost every trace of her sister.

Did it fail because I was alone?

Ruth had been on her own on the night of the fire, and it had worked for her. Emily puzzled over this mystery during breakfast, and on the drive to school. John's instructions said two people were required. It was possible, however, that he'd been talking about the actual making of the potion, which Emily had helped with.

Maybe it didn't work last night because Ruth didn't know about it.

But Ruth would never agree to casting the spell again. Emily needed to find someone else so that they could brew the stuff up from scratch. Someone who understood Smockeroon.

★

Emily got to her classroom more than ten minutes before the bell.

Maze was here at her desk – without Summer.

'Hi,' Emily said uncertainly.

Maze scowled. 'Just stop it, will you?'

'What are you talking about? I haven't—'

'Very funny!' hissed Maze. 'Don't pretend you don't know!' She shoved a dirty scrap of paper into Emily's hand. 'I don't know how you sneaked it into my pocket – but if it happens again . . .'

Summer Watson made her entrance at this moment, and Maze pointedly turned her back. This was still hurtful, and a couple of weeks ago Emily would have felt like crying. Now she was just annoyed. She glanced at the note.

HaHAHAHA YoU are a BUM and I wiLL BOPE yOu!

Prison Wendy again. The word 'Bope' came as a slight shock. Years ago, at nursery school, boping had been one of Prizzy's naughty inventions. When you 'boped' someone, you put your hands on their cheeks and squished their face. Emily and Maze had found it hilarious; they had boped each other until the boping craze had spread around the whole nursery – and then Maze's parents, tired of being boped, had banned it, and sent Prizzy back to her box on the top shelf. Now the awful doll was back in the community and thirsting for trouble; was it possible that the broken barrier between the worlds had made her even worse?

Martha rushed in late, when Ms Robinson was already halfway through the register.

'Sorry, sorry, sorry!' She was pink and flustered, and her curly hair had taken on a life of its own. 'We got stuck behind a broken-down lorry full of cows.'

'Sit down and get your breath back,' said Ms

Robinson. 'And try to remember this when you're playing the White Rabbit.'

A small yellow head popped suddenly out of the front pocket of Martha's backpack. 'Hi, Emily!'

'Hi, Pippa.' Emily said it without thinking – and got a very odd look from Martha, almost as if she were frightened. Could she hear?

There wasn't time to talk now. This morning they had school assembly, when the whole of Hatty Catty packed themselves into the enormous hall. The Headmistress, Mrs Willis, read out notices and showed some photos of her recent visit to Nigeria. Most of the pictures were of schools and teachers.

'Huh – call that a holiday?' shrilled a familiar voice. 'Bor-ing!'

Emily froze; how had Pippa got out of Martha's bag?

Mrs Willis, hearing nothing, showed a picture of herself in traditional African dress; her normal clothes were very plain and dowdy, and there was some giggling over how she looked in a long gown covered with red and gold flowers.

'Ooh, isn't that lovely?' squeaked Pippa. 'Can I have a pink one? Martha, it's even prettier than your flowery knickers!'

Martha's face was bright red – and that was when Emily knew for sure.

She can hear.

★

'It started last night,' said Martha. 'I was just getting into bed when she suddenly jumped out of my school bag and started singing and dancing.'

'What did you do – were you shocked?'

'Are you kidding? I nearly passed out!'

'And that was the first time?' It was morning break. Emily had dragged Martha off to the remotest part of the school grounds, an unpopular windy bench beside a section of wire fence, where they could talk properly.

'Yes – and when I woke up this morning I told myself it must've been a dream,' said Martha. 'But then she was off again. She started singing inside my bag while I was eating breakfast, and she wouldn't shut up in the car when Dad was driving me to school. I'm so glad someone else can hear her and it's not just me!' She smiled suddenly, light breaking over her sweet, round (slightly toyish) face. 'I don't mind being crazy if I've got company.'

'You're not crazy,' said Emily. 'I can't explain it all now but I need your help with something. Can you come back with me this afternoon?'

If Martha helps me, I won't need Ruth.

'OK – I'll text my mum.'

'Good morning, Emily!' A tiny yellow head emerged from the front pocket of Molly's bag. 'Isn't this fun?'

'I wish you'd keep out of sight,' said Martha.

'Hi Pippa,' said Emily. 'Shouldn't you be at the Seam-Rite factory?'

'I've decided to take a holiday,' said Pippa. 'I've always wanted to visit a real human big school. When can I see a lesson?'

'Sorry, Pips.' Martha pushed Pippa back out of sight and firmly zipped her in. 'Lessons are strictly humans only.'

The little bear was very annoyed and there were a few minutes of muffled shouting before she suddenly went quiet.

'I think she's gone.' Emily gave the bag an experimental squeeze. 'She feels like a toy again.'

'Good,' said Martha. She was thoughtful. They sat in silence for a few minutes, listening to the reassuringly ordinary noises of voices and traffic. 'This the weirdest thing that's ever happened to me.'

'Me too.'

'You know, when I was little I would've loved my toys to come to life and talk to me. And I did think Pippa looked tremendously sweet when she was moving and talking. But I was mainly scared – well, not scared. Sort of nervous, like when you're afraid of mice. It's not only Pippa, is it?'

'No.'

'So what's going on?'

'I don't know.'

'And – why?'

'I don't know.' Emily wasn't being totally truthful, but her own idea was too far-fetched to say out loud.

It's all happening because two sisters refused to be parted.

Seventeen

THE SPELLBINDERS

THE MAD STORY of Smockeroon poured out as soon as they were alone together in Emily's bedroom, with the door firmly shut. Martha was a wonderful audience, and thanks to Pippa, she believed every word of it.

'If I go next door, will I be able to see Notty and John Staples' old toys? I love his books so much! Will I be able to talk to them?'

'I think you will,' said Emily. 'But you mustn't tell Ruth about the potion. She meant to throw it away. She'll be really cross if she finds out I've been fiddling with it. We're supposed to be fixing the leak, because it's letting sadness into Smockeroon – and of course I want to fix it, and find the Sturvey. But before that happens, the door's still open. And that means there's still a chance that I can get in.'

'You said it didn't work when you tried it.' Martha picked up the plastic bottle and swished the dirty water; she was doubtful but also excited, and intensely curious.

'That batch didn't work for me because Ruth was the chief spellbinder,' said Emily. 'That's my theory, anyway.'

'So you need to make some more – do you remember the recipe?'

'Yes.'

'Can we do it today?'

'It's . . . complicated.'

Emily had to be honest about the danger involved. Ruth had nearly died. 'I know the official reason for the fire was an electrical fault. But Ruth says the fact that we'd just cast the spell was too much of a coincidence, and we mustn't take any more risks.'

Martha listened carefully as Emily told her the full story of that night, ending with the sudden intervention of the German lodger.

'You were OK, though.'

'Yes,' said Emily. 'I wasn't the chief spellbinder.

It's fine if you're just the assistant – and that's all I'm asking you to do. I wouldn't ask if I thought I was putting you in danger.' (She hoped this was true.) 'It's just a tiny bit of chanting. Honestly.'

She wanted to beg and plead, but forced herself to keep quiet while Martha made up her mind. The silence seemed to stretch on for ages. Martha stared at the plastic bottle, and at first her fresh, round face was fearful. But Emily could see that she was also incredibly excited – and the excitement was winning.

'Would I get to see toys' TV?'

'Maybe,' said Emily. 'I don't see why not; you're just as good at seeing magic stuff as I am, and I was only assistant spellbinder when I saw it.'

'Wow.' Martha was tempted. 'And I've just thought of something. If you get to Smockeroon, and I can watch you on TV, that would mean I'd be standing by if the German lodger sees another fire or something.'

'So you could – that's a fantastic idea!' said Emily, grabbing at it eagerly. 'You'd be awake in the hard world, and you can raise the alarm if you see or hear that I'm in danger!'

'What kind of danger should I be looking out for?' asked Martha, doubtful again.

'Nothing criminal, or violent.' Emily swallowed a couple of times to stop her voice quivering with impatience. 'One of the toys will warn you, like the German lodger warned me. You don't need to worry unless you see me going too far into the background.'

'Background?'

'Deep Smockeroon: you can only see it in the distance, and Ruth thinks humans can't get there unless they're dead.'

'Oh,' said Martha, catching her breath. 'But you won't be allowed to go that deep. You'll just have to keep reminding yourself to stay near The Sycamores.'

'I'll play it safe, I promise.'

'OK,' Martha said slowly. 'I'm up for it.'

'Thanks – and I swear you won't be in any danger.'

'Actually, I'd love to be part of this. I'm already part of it, thanks to Pippa!' Martha was smiling again. 'So ... when do we make our witch's brew? Now?'

'We have to wait till my parents are out of the way,' said Emily, coming down to earth a little as she faced the practicalities. 'And they're always hanging about in the kitchen. Could we do it at your house?'

'Sorry,' said Martha. 'Our kitchen's never empty.

And my mum doesn't like me messing about with her saucepans.'

'Oh.' This was frustrating; how could they cast their spell without making the parents suspicious? 'I can't believe it's so complicated when we only need a few minutes!' Emily, sitting on her bed, slumped crossly against the wall.

'Wait a minute!' Martha's face lit up suddenly. 'I've had a brilliant idea!' She was sitting at the desk in the swivel chair, and she spun round in it gleefully. 'We can do it at my sleepover!'

'What – in front of everybody?'

'No, of course not.' Martha stopped spinning and became businesslike. 'We're holding the party in our barn, the one that's used as a wedding venue – and it's got a little kitchen!'

'But there'll be crowds of people—' began Emily.

'We'll wait till the disco, when it's dark. Or when everyone else is asleep – don't you see?' She spun round again, until her face was an excited blur. 'Perfect!'

'Yes, but someone's bound to come crashing in while we're waiting for the saucepan to heat up! It takes a lot longer than you think.'

'We won't need a saucepan,' Martha sang out happily. 'There isn't a stove – just a microwave!'

'But that won't work!'

Martha stopped her spinning again. 'Why not? The spell just says to heat the water. It doesn't specify how.'

★

By Saturday afternoon – the day of the sleepover – Emily was seething with impatience to try the spell again. Would it work with a microwave? She would have liked to experiment with heating the water, to see how long it would take. But her mother would never allow her to play about with boiling water. And the toys had been dismayingly quiet since Pippa's inconvenient appearance at school, even the three old Staples toys.

'I haven't heard a single thing for days,' Ruth had said yesterday. 'Maybe they've found the Sturvey and it's all over?'

Emily had pretended to think this was good news, but was secretly worried; what if she had missed her chance to get to Smockeroon? While she was packing her rucksack, she took special care with the tiny plastic bag that contained the stuff they would need to make the potion – ten blades of grass, meticulously measured, and a needle she had swiped from her mother's sewing box. She had also raided the medicine drawer for a sticking plaster, to use after she had pricked her thumb.

'Em, are you ready?' Dad called upstairs. 'You said you wanted to be early.'

'Just a sec!' Emily zipped up her backpack and suddenly caught her reflection in the mirror – still in jeans and sweatshirt, her hair in a total mess.

She was going to a party.

I can't turn up like this!

She hadn't thought about clothes since Holly died. For a few minutes she blundered around her room in a panic, until she remembered the only dress she owned that still fitted – stretchy purple velvet, one of her birthday presents. It was crumpled into a corner of the wardrobe, but it was clean and the creases quickly fell out. She ripped off the jeans and sweatshirt, pulled on a pair of black school tights and hastily wriggled her way into the dress.

'Emily!'

'I'm coming!'

Her black school shoes were boring, and made her feet look gigantic, but her only other shoes were trainers. She dragged a brush though her long hair and dared to look in the mirror again. For one scalding second, she saw a purple idiot with a weird pointed nose and feet like two tugboats – but when she had taken a couple of breaths, she could see that she looked fine. Nice, even.

'Em! What're you doing up there?'

'I'm getting dressed!'

Emily remembered her best necklace; the long string of blue glass beads that Holly had liked for the clinking noise they made. She put this on, and the matching bracelet. As an afterthought, just on the point of running downstairs, she grabbed the Bluey book from her beside table. This would be the first time she'd spent a night away from home since Holly died, and she didn't feel right about leaving it behind.

Dad stopped mid shout when he saw Emily, and whistled instead. 'You're gorgeous!'

'You look lovely!' Mum hugged her. 'Have a great time.'

★

198

The farm where Martha lived was a few miles outside Barkstone, at the end of a long country lane. Dad winced as the car rattled over the cattle grids, and said it was a good thing there was a map on the back of the invitation.

They were early, but the big muddy yard in front of the shabby farmhouse was already filling up with cars, girls and parents. Three muddy dogs circled about eagerly, trying to cover the guests with paw marks.

'Hi, Emily – you look fantastic!' Martha (in a bright pink dress and matching lipstick) jumped out of the chaos to hug her, and hissed into her ear, 'Did you bring it – are we still on?'

'Yes,' Emily whispered back. 'I'll be waiting for your sign.'

They exchanged secret gleeful smiles, and then Emily said, in a normal voice, 'Happy birthday and I love your dress.'

The Ambers arrived, along with several other girls from school, and there was more hugging. The party had started. Nothing could happen until darkness had fallen and everyone else was distracted, so Emily shoved the spellbinding to the back of her mind;

there was no reason why she couldn't enjoy herself in the meantime.

By the time Dad drove away, she had remembered the feeling of having fun – shouting, dancing, eating, laughing. It was ages since she'd been to a sleepover and Martha's family had pulled out all the stops with this one. They were all going to sleep together in the barn that had been turned into an enormous party room and wedding venue. There was karaoke and a disco with Uncle Mike (fully clothed) as DJ.

When the disco was at its height, Martha – wildly excited – tugged at Emily's sleeve and the two of them wove through the crowd of thrashing, dancing bodies. It was easy, in the confusion of flashing disco lights, to sneak into the tiny kitchen at the back of the barn. They couldn't see each other properly, or hear each other through the thump-thump-thump of the music, until Martha had switched on the light and closed the door.

'OK, I've got all the stuff.' Emily fished the tiny plastic bag out of her sleeve. 'Nobody will miss us, will they?'

'No – Mum's not bringing in my cake until the end of 'The Birdie Song'. Hurry up!'

The cramped space contained only a small metal sink, a couple of cupboards and the microwave. The plastic measuring jug, containing precisely one pint of water, was already waiting inside the microwave for its first blast of heat.

It was a tricky operation. Martha leaned close to the glass door, watching the jug of water. The first bubbles appeared; they took the jug out of the microwave just long enough for Emily to drop in the blades of grass and stab the needle into her thumb (it hurt a lot) for a drop of blood. Together, they chanted, 'To Smockeroon! Smockeroon! Smockeroon!'

'It'll be cool enough for you to drink by the time we go to sleep,' said Martha. 'I wish I could drink it too. I know, I know, you don't need to say it again – but I hope I get to see something!'

They went back to the party. Uncle Mike finished the disco and Martha's mother brought in a magnificent pink-and-silver birthday cake, decked with sparklers and so huge it had to be wheeled on a trolley.

Emily sang 'Happy Birthday' with everyone else and did her best to ignore her prickling impatience to find out if their microwaved potion worked.

Finally, well after midnight, the party guests began to climb into their sleeping bags, and Emily darted back to the tiny kitchen; the water in the jug was still warm and there was no way she could carry it back to her sleeping place on the floor beside Martha, so she kept the spoonful of mixture in her mouth and didn't swallow it until she was lying down. She put her arms by her side, and muttered the rhyme, 'Magic mountain, rivers deep . . .'

'If something happens and I'm still asleep,' Martha gabbled into her ear, 'wake me up – pinch me as hard as you like!'

Martha's mother handed out mugs of hot chocolate and turned off the main lights.

Everyone said they were going to stay awake all night.

Ten minutes later they were all soundly asleep – including Emily.

The next thing she knew, someone was shaking her shoulder.

'Emily, wake up! You have to see this!'

'What?' Emily sat up blearily. 'The spell—'

'It worked!'

Emily blinked a couple of times, cross with herself for falling asleep. The still, silent shapes of the other party guests were bathed in a strange white light, soft yet intense; she couldn't work out where it was coming from, until Martha – in such a state of excitement that she forgot to whisper – cried out, 'Can't you see? It's coming from your bag!'

Emily's blue backpack, a few feet away, was filled with the mysterious light; it glowed though the seams and poured out of the zipped pockets, as if someone had tried to bag up the moon.

'Careful – it might be hot.'

The blue nylon felt slightly warm when Emily dragged it towards her and started pulling out the things inside – washbag, non-party clothes, phone. She touched the secret pocket where she kept the Bluey book; it was hot without being uncomfortable, like bathwater, and when she unzipped it, the sudden rush of light made them both screw up their eyes.

And then there was a sudden sunburst of magic, multicoloured glitter, and a chorus of toyish voices:

'HAPPY BIRTHDAY MARTHA!'

It was an incredible and unforgettable sight. Dozens of pretty toys and dolls in sequinned hats marched two-by-two through the sleeping partygoers, singing loudly:

We are the Seam-Rite Girls –
Won't you join our song?
Our Seam-Rite cream
Works like a dream
And lasts the whole day long!

The Seam-Rite Girls curtseyed and Emily and Martha clapped.

'Oh, they're so gorgeous!' Martha was in ecstasy. 'But why's everyone asleep?'

The bright, glittering light showed that all the other party guests were in such a deep sleep that they did not stir when toys trooped across their bodies.

Pippa jumped onto the nearby head of Amber Frost. 'Did you like it? We've been practising for days!'

'Thanks, Pips, I loved it,' said Martha.

PARP-PARP!

The rough, blaring sound ripped through the room and several toys screamed.

And then a rude voice yelled out, 'How's that for a novelty fart?'

Suddenly, out of nowhere, more toys were marching through the party barn – a long, straggling line of very

dirty, shabby rag dolls, who were singing in loud,
rude voices:

You are the Seam-Rite bums –
So stuck-up and so mean!
You needn't think you are so great
Just because you're clean!

Some of these rag dolls were bald, some had
missing arms or legs, some had leaking stuffing – the
Seam-Rite Girls backed away from them in horror.

And then a voice rang out that stirred up a very
old memory.

'Hello Emily!'

This doll was a bundle of rags – more rags than
doll – with two mouldy plaits of red wool and a
drawn-on face with a mad, wonky grin.

'Prizzy!' gasped Emily. 'What are you doing here?'

Prison Wendy folded her arms and did the 'naughty
dance' invented for her by four-year-old Maze.

'Stop doing the dance.' Emily suddenly remembered
how to talk to the famous jailbird. 'Go away at once!'

'NO!' yelled Prizzy. 'We want to be Seam-Rite
Girls and they won't let us!'

Squeaks of horror rippled through the Seam-Rite toys.

'Don't be ridiculous!' Pippa stamped angrily on the sleeping face of Amber Frost. 'You're far too dirty and smelly! Now stop spoiling my human's party.'

'NO!' Prizzy turned to face her ragged companions. 'OK, ladies – you know what to do!'

With a horrible quickness, the dirty rag dolls suddenly scuttled over the sleeping bags and leapt on top of Pippa.

'HELP!' screamed the yellow bear. 'MARTHA – HELP!'

'Stop it – put her down at once!' Emily made a grab at the filthy, wriggling heap, but they were too quick for her. She had one glimpse of Pippa with a sack over her head—

And then all the toys vanished, and a lone voice rang out. 'Make us Seam-Rite Girls – *or we'll turn her into one of us!*'

The barn was dark again. The two girls sat for a moment in silence, shocked and bewildered by what they had just seen.

Martha whispered, 'They've kidnapped Pippa!'

Eighteen

FIREWORKS

'PIPS IS HERE – but she's not here.' Martha prodded the small yellow bear. 'Even when she's a normal stuffed toy, her face shows a bit of her personality. Now she just looks empty, as if she'd never been imagined.'

'That's how we know she was kidnapped,' said Emily.

It was the Monday afternoon after the sleepover and the beginning of half-term. Emily had invited Martha for tea and they had dropped into the antique shop to tell Ruth the whole story – including the secret experiment they had done with the potion (it was a great relief to come clean about this).

'And it was definitely Prison Wendy?' Ruth frowned thoughtfully at the 'empty' Pippa on her table beside the till.

'Yes,' said Emily. 'I'd know her anywhere. You have to believe us.'

'Oh, I believe you – I don't understand how it's possible, that's all. Let me get it straight. Your old friend wants to be a Seam-Rite Girl, or she'll make Pippa as dirty as she is?'

Emily and Martha nodded; they were all very serious. This was yet another sign of the nastiness that had infected Smockeroon.

'What does Prizzy think you can do about it – phone the Seam-Rite factory?'

Notty's voice floated down from the shelf. 'You could send off for an application form. The fact remains, however, that the rules are very strict – clean, pretty toys only.'

'That's not fair!' Emily was surprised to feel a stab of sympathy for Prizzy. 'Why shouldn't she be a Seam-Rite Girl, if that's what she wants? In my stories for Holly, toys could be anything they liked. This goes against the laws of Smockeroon.'

'Blame the toad,' said Notty. 'That wretched creature brought all this naughtiness into our peaceful land. I'm sure you heard about the theft at The Sycamores – the whole top floor! Hugo was

208

simply furious. If you haven't seen him for a few days it because he's busy rebuilding.'

'Poor old Hugo!' Ruth shook her head sorrowfully. 'It hurts so much to think of Danny's toys being sad. I'd never have told him a story like this. There must be something we can do.'

Emily asked, 'Is it partly my fault, because of the potion?'

'I doubt it,' said Ruth. 'But I do wish you hadn't mucked about with John's magic. It can't be safe. Please promise not to do it again.'

'OK.'

I promise not to do that particular spell again.

I don't promise to give up trying to see Holly and Bluey.

A loud BANG outside brought them back to the hard world; Podge twitched and yowled under the desk.

'Dear old cat!' Ruth bent down to stroke his head. 'Firework night starts earlier every year and he hates all the explosions.'

'So do our dogs,' said Martha. 'They go berserk and we have to shut them in the boot room. We can only have fireworks that don't bang.'

'Yes, us too,' said Emily. 'Because Holly—' She nearly said, 'Because Holly doesn't like the noise.'

This time last year, Emily had spent the whole evening of Bonfire Night singing Bluey songs softly into Holly's ear, and stroking her cheek with Bluey's paw. Mum had said it really helped.

'It's awful when the anniversaries come round,' Ruth said. 'And you can't stop thinking, this time last year. It made me so sad that things like fireworks and Christmas could carry on happening when Danny wasn't there. Time is cruel. It keeps moving me further away from him.' She was quiet for a few moments. 'You know, if you want to rescue Pippa, maybe you should find Prison Wendy in the hard world.'

'But she's at Maze's,' said Emily. 'I'd have to get myself invited to her house.'

'She'll probably be at the bonfire party on the common,' said Martha. 'Her mum always does the cake stall.'

Barkstone Common was a large, scrubby piece of land on the outskirts of the old village. Every year there was a huge bonfire, spectacular fireworks and delicious food that was sold to raise money for the hospital. Emily had been a few times with Maze and her parents, but for the last few years she had been too worried about Holly to leave home. Now she needed to be there; it could be her one chance to talk to Maze outside school.

That evening, while they were having supper, Emily said, trying to sound casual, 'Martha wants me to go to the bonfire thing. Her dad's doing the barbecue.'

'As a matter of fact,' Mum said, 'I promised Jo Miller I'd bring a few cakes and help out on the stall.'

'So . . . we're going?'

'It sounds like fun,' Mum said. 'And I thought it would be better than staying at home and remembering.'

★

The bonfire party began as soon as the clear, pale sky turned deep, inky blue. It was very cold. Emily and her mother had a slight argument when Mum noticed that Emily wasn't wearing a hat; Emily couldn't tell her that the only warm hat she'd been able to find had belonged to Holly. They arrived early with Mum's boxes of cakes, and the huge fire, tall as a house, had only just been lit. The air had an exciting tang

211

of smoke and people were black outlines against the flickering orange flames.

Maze's mother had set up her food tables a good distance away from the fire; she was very glad to see the boxes of cakes.

'These look brilliant – thanks so much! Are you sure you don't mind doing a stint behind the stall?'

'Not at all,' Mum said, brightening up because she loved doing things like this. 'Em, why don't you and Maze grab something from the barbecue, before the queue gets too long?'

Maze and Emily looked at each other. There was no point in arguing; their mothers thought they were still friends. In silence they walked off together across the uneven, lumpy grass, towards the flock of people around the barbecue. Emily had to stick close to Maze; it was very dark now and Maze had a torch. A rocket soared over them in a whoosh of stars.

The silence between them went on for ages, until Emily couldn't stand it.

'Where's Summer?'

Maze was suspicious – she took a moment to check that Emily wasn't being snide. 'She had to stay at home. They're having a big party.'

'Oh.'

'Of course she asked me to the party,' Maze said furiously. 'But Mum said I had to come to this lame thing instead. To be supportive.'

'Oh,' Emily said again.

'I bet you're pleased.'

'Come on, Maze! Why would I be pleased?'

'Well . . .' Maze was less confident without Summer. 'Because you're jealous.'

'Maze, I didn't send those notes. You know who sent them.'

'Don't be stupid!' She was nervous now. 'It's messing with my head. You're weird. And it's even getting into my dreams!'

'What did you dream about?' This was hopeful; if Maze had started to have dreams about the toys, maybe she'd stop blaming Emily for the notes.

'Nothing!' Maze's anger was edged with fear. 'Leave me alone!'

Emily bit back a storm of questions. They had walked into the pool of light around the barbecue and there was already a short queue. Martha's dad waved to Emily. He wore a plastic apron that said 'MASTER'.

'Hi, Emily!' Martha stood beside him; her apron said 'SLAVE'. 'Hi, Maze – burger or sausage?'

The fireworks were getting louder now and the huge bonfire threw a confusing, flickering orange light across the crowd. A rocket screeched over their heads in a white flash. For one moment, Emily thought she saw something moving on the grass, like a flock of small animals – but when the next flash came there was nothing.

I'm just being paranoid.

'Ketchup and mustard down the end!' Martha handed them each hot dogs smothered with fried onions. 'Yum, don't you love this smell? I've already had two of these.'

It's difficult to keep up an argument, or even a conversation, when you're eating a hot dog. Emily and Maze stood together, a few feet from the barbecue, wolfing down the (fantastic) hot dogs and gazing at the fireworks, in a silence that was almost companionable. Emily sensed that Maze was getting her temper back – she had always been a pushover for barbecue food.

Does this mean we might be friends again?

It couldn't ever be exactly the same between

them – they had both moved on. But there was no reason why they couldn't have a few laughs together. Emily had missed Maze's crazy sense of humour.

She knew all Holly's favourite noises.

Emily didn't want to be the first to speak.

But of course – she knew her so well – Maze had to do everything first. She gobbled down her hot dog long before Emily had finished hers. 'That was gorgeous! At Summer's they're having chicken satay – but I'd much rather have this, wouldn't you?'

Something shifted between them, like an invisible wall falling down; suddenly, just like that, it was all right. If this was the old Maze, it might not be so difficult to tell her a totally far-fetched story about toys.

Your old doll has kidnapped Martha's bear.

Of course it sounded ridiculous. Emily and Martha had agreed not to tell Maze anything until Martha had finished helping with the barbecue and they could do it together.

'OK, I'm free now.' Martha appeared beside them out of the darkness. 'Let's go to the cake stall. My mum's doing mugs of hot chocolate.'

'Stop right there!' a weird little voice squeaked

suddenly. 'You haven't heard our demands— Ouch – drat – I'm all tangled!'

Something moved violently in the folds of the striped scarf around Martha's neck.

'What—?' Maze watched, thunderstruck, as a small yellow head poked out.

'Pips!' cried Martha. 'You're here – you're back!' She grabbed her bear and held her tightly. 'I was so worried! I thought you'd been kidnapped!'

'Oh, yes,' said Pippa. 'But that's all over. My so-called kidnappers told me their terrible story, and now I'm on their side.' Her furry face squished into a proud smile. 'They made me their leader and now I live with them and I showed them how to make nice curtains. Please tell Hugo I won't be coming back to The Sycamores and I'm sorry about the top floor.'

'You mean – that was you?' Emily was surprised and uneasy; this did not sound right coming from the stitched mouth of sweet little Pippa. 'You're the criminal who stole the top floor of The Sycamores?'

'All my things were in there and I couldn't be bothered to pack,' Pippa said airily. 'I was too busy organising the demo.'

Maze let out a strange rasping sound; the firework flashes gave Emily snapshots of her astonished face.

And then a great shout rose up from the ground around their feet.

'WHAT DO WE WANT?'

'BETTER HUMANS!'

'WHEN DO WE WANT THEM?'

'NOW!'

The shouting came from a large crowd of very dirty, battered rag dolls. Some of them were holding up placards that read:

'NEW HAIR FOR ALL!'

'WASH MY FACE!'

'STUFF ME NOW!'

Maze looked as if she might faint. She clutched Emily's arm. 'What is this? What's going on?'

'It's a PROTEST MARCH!' roared a familiar voice.

A single bundle of rags detached itself from the filthy crowd and scuttled across the grass.

'Prizzy!' choked Maze.

'Hello, Maze!' said Prizzy.

Nineteen

DEMANDS

FOR ONCE IN HER LIFE, Maze was speechless.
      'Prizzy, go away,' said Emily. 'This is a party for humans – get back to your own dimension.'

'NO!' shouted Prizzy. 'Not until you've heard our DEMANDS! Now the Sturvey's disappeared, NO ONE CAN STOP US!'

The ragged rabble behind her broke out in angry shouts.

'I don't think anybody else can see them.' Martha glanced around at the other humans. 'Or hear them. Nobody seems to have noticed a thing!'

'Tell them, Prizzy!' called Pippa. 'Don't let the humans put you off!'

'OK,' said Prizzy. 'Maze Miller, you have

twenty-four hours to mend me!' She waved a grubby scrap of paper. 'Here's my list of demands.'

Emily bent down to take it. There was just enough light to read the wiggling lines of purple crayon.

1. New HARE
2. A new FASE that doesn't look barmy
3. A NEW dres
4. Some little gold boots.

'Hear hear!' yelled someone in the crowd.

There were shouts of 'MEND HER!'

'Things have changed in Smockeroon,' said Pippa, wriggling impatiently in her owner's gloved hand. 'Now we can TALK BACK!'

'Come on,' Emily said, doing her best to sound reasonable. 'You know Maze can't do all that!'

'Twenty-four hours,' Prizzy repeated grimly. 'I know how to fix that broken door. But if you don't mend me, I'M THROWING IT WIDE OPEN!'

The angry dolls suddenly disappeared and Pippa turned back into an ordinary stuffed toy.

It was a normal fireworks party again. Emily, Maze and Martha stared into each other's shocked faces.

'Broken door?' Maze whispered. 'What's she talking about?'

'It's quite a long story.' Emily had never seen her former best friend so rattled, and this distracted her from thinking about the dreadful Prizzy and her demands. 'Are you OK?'

'I . . . I don't know. How did you do that?'

'You look like you're going to pass out,' said Martha. 'Let's get some hot chocolate.'

The three of them – Martha and Emily dragging Maze between them – went over to where Martha's mother was doing a brisk trade in her mugs of hot chocolate.

'Hi, girls!' Ruth waved to them from one of the tables outside the pub, where she had been watching the fireworks with two friends from the book club. They had just gone, leaving a crowd of wine glasses.

Martha said, 'I wonder if she saw anything?'

It was a relief to sit down at the table with Ruth, who kindly moved a few glasses to make room for their mugs. Emily (with interruptions from Martha) spilled out the story of the ragged protest march and Prizzy's terrible threat.

Ruth listened very seriously. 'So little Pippa's gone

over to the other side – I didn't know toys could get Stockholm Syndrome!' She quickly added, seeing that nobody knew what this was, 'That's what they call it when a kidnapped person starts to identify with their kidnappers. And as for Prizzy and her cheeky demands, I certainly didn't know toys could be blackmailers.'

'She gave us twenty-four hours,' Emily said. 'And then she disappeared before I could make her see that it's totally impossible – I mean, where are we supposed to get those gold boots?'

'I don't think you should panic about the twenty-four hours,' said Ruth. 'Toys are rubbish at telling the time – well, look at all the trouble Hugo and Smiffy had with that cuckoo. Maze, you imagined Prison Wendy. Could she tell the time?'

Maze had stopped looking ill. She was now in equal parts fascinated and bewildered. 'No, she wasn't clever enough. And anyway, I couldn't tell the time myself back then – I was only four.'

'Just as I thought.' Ruth nodded wisely. 'When she turns up we'll simply tell her she's early.'

'I'm sorry, I don't get it,' Maze said. 'I don't understand the stuff about the broken door – why is it such a big deal?'

'Because the wrong things are getting into the wrong worlds,' Ruth said. 'Terrible silliness is about to invade the hard world, which is bad when this world is complicated and needs to be managed by people who haven't been stuffed. But something much nastier has got into Smockeroon.'

Emily remembered, with a chill of foreboding, the evening of the book group, and how creepy it had felt to be the only non-silly person present. 'Is there anything we can do?'

'We could try giving in to Prizzy's demands.' Ruth looked at Maze. 'Bring her round to me and I'll tidy her up a bit – that should buy us some more time.'

'But I can't,' Maze said helplessly. 'I don't know where she is!'

★

There was no chance to search for Prison Wendy properly until after school on the following Tuesday, when Maze brought Emily and Martha back to tea at her house.

'Summer's really cross with me,' Maze said

gloomily. 'She wanted me to come back with her today, and she wouldn't believe any of my excuses.'

'Maybe you should've told her the truth,' said Martha.

'She'd never listen. She thinks toys are lame. All her old toys got thrown away. Now she's ignoring me.'

Emily knew how this felt, and was slightly (only slightly) sorry for her. Now it was her turn for the invisible treatment. 'It won't take long. All we need to do is find Prizzy and give her to Ruth. How hard can it be?'

Before Holly died, Emily had practically lived at Maze's house. It was a shock to realise now that she hadn't been there since the day at the end of the holidays, when Mum and Dad had sent her to Maze's so she wouldn't have to watch the men ripping out Holly's chairlift.

Maze's mother said, as she pulled up in the drive, 'Welcome back, Emily – we've missed you!'

There was no time to feel awkward. They had already made plans.

'Mum, do you mind if we go in the garage?' Maze did her best to sound casual. 'I swear we won't make a mess.'

'We're looking for something,' Martha added.

'You won't find anything there. It's full of all the guilty rubbish I don't know what to do with. And it's covered with dust.' Maze's mother was suspicious. 'Don't you want to take Emily and Martha up to your room?'

'In a minute. We just need to look.'

They dumped their bags and school blazers in the hall and Maze opened the door that led into the garage. She switched on the light. The three of them stood for a moment in glum silence.

Maze groaned. 'This is going to be impossible.'

It certainly did look pretty hopeless. There was no space here for even a small car. The Millers' garage was crammed with junk – two broken lawnmowers, an old exercise bike, and boxes, boxes, boxes, piled up to the ceiling.

And it was freezing cold. Emily shivered and hugged herself. Bluey seemed further off than ever. 'Are you sure she's in here?'

'No! I've been trying and trying to remember when my old toys got put here – I think it was when the house got painted. Mum wouldn't chuck anything out without telling me.'

'You're not thinking magically,' said Martha. 'Prizzy! Tell us where you are!'

Silence.

'This is stupid,' said Maze.

'Prizzy!' Emily called, trying to sound firm (and feeling a bit of an idiot in front of Maze). 'Stop being naughty – you're the one who told us to come here!'

A rude voice said, 'NO! Hahaha!'

She was here – a look of triumph flashed between the girls.

'You have a go.' Emily nudged Maze. 'You're her human. She has to listen to you.'

'Er – Prizzy . . .' began Maze. 'Tell us where you are . . . at once!'

'NO!'

'Leave this to me,' said Martha. 'Prizzy, if you don't come out and show yourself, how can I measure your feet for those gold boots?'

Emily mouthed, 'What?'

'I found some gold material in the bag for the jumble sale,' Martha whispered. 'I'm sure Ruth can make some little boots with it – shhh!'

There was a rustling, scuffling noise and a dirty

little head suddenly appeared at the top of a teetering pile of cardboard boxes.

'Gold boots!' Prizzy's bonkers face was filled with joy. 'My dream has come true!'

In a few wild leaps, she launched herself neatly into Maze's arms.

'Wow – how did you do that?' Maze held the filthy little creature at arm's length, and suddenly started laughing. 'She totally ignored me, but she listened to you.'

'I think Martha's a natural toy whisperer,' said Emily. 'I think some people have a special talent for talking to toys. It's something they're just born with – like a good singing voice, or blue eyes. It's why Pippa chose her.'

'Wow.' Maze stared at her old doll and suddenly smiled. 'I can't take all the blame for Prizzy being so naughty. You invented at least half of her – your imagination's a lot better than mine. Actually, I've missed the way you're always making up stories.'

'Thanks.' Emily was pleased; it was good to know that Maze had not forgotten.

'Summer won't talk about anything except celebrities,' said Maze. 'It gets a bit boring and she goes all snide when I get them mixed up. But they all look the same – bright orange with weird mouths – and I can't always tell them apart.'

'There's a gale-force wind blowing directly up my skirt,' said Martha. 'Let's get back to the warm. We can do Mrs Lewis's homework and nick the answers off each other.'

Prizzy was a limp bundle of rags now. Five minutes later they were sitting cosily around the Millers' kitchen table like three normal, non-magic girls.

Twenty

GOLD BOOTS

'Summer's furious with me,' said Maze. 'She doesn't understand why I have to go back with you again, when I did it only yesterday. I tried telling her that my mum had ordered me – but all she said was, "Since when did you listen to her?" And then she went off with that stupid Laura Brady and spent the whole day whispering with her. And I know for a fact that she doesn't even like Laura.'

Maze had not had a good day and was very downcast.

Of course Emily knew exactly how she felt – but her dad would have said, 'Get my smallest violin,' meaning he was sorry but not all that sorry.

I didn't have anyone – and she's got us.

'Never mind,' said Martha. 'You've always got us.'

'*Argh!* Saddled with you two – this is social doom!' Maze was suddenly joking again. 'Aren't you dying to see what Ruth's done with Prizzy?'

'Whatever it is,' Emily said, 'we have to say she looks divinely beautiful – if we get her into a good mood, we might be able to convince her to help us fix the door.'

The three of them were waiting in the after-school chaos of girls, bikes and cars around the main entrance. Emily's mother arrived, and (as Emily had predicted) was delighted that she was bringing back two friends.

'It's fine by me, if it's OK with your parents. I knew I made that lemon drizzle cake for a reason!'

'Yum!' Maze smiled greedily. 'My favourite!'

They couldn't talk about the toys in front of Emily's mother. But there was plenty to talk about in the car, as she had volunteered to work on the costumes for the play. Alongside Emily's Alice dress, she was making an elaborate Tudor gown for Maze, just like the illustrations of the Red Queen in the book. Emily was still nervous about the play, but starting to be excited. They were doing two full-scale performances – one for the whole school, and another on the following evening for parents and friends.

'I'm terrified,' said Maze (who was not terrified). 'Every time I think of that huge hall and the sea of faces in front of me.'

Emily pushed this scary picture out of her mind and began to think about Prizzy's makeover – was it actually possible to make her look anything like a normal rag doll? And (far more important) did she really know how to break the barrier between the two worlds? Of course the door must be fixed, but there had to be a chance to see Bluey first.

The three girls hurried straight round to Ruth's, the moment they got home (Emily had told her mother a mild lie about Ruth helping with a school project). She was waiting in her chair behind the till.

'Turn the sign round.'

Emily turned the sign on the door from 'Open' to 'Closed'.

'Notty – you can talk now,' said Ruth, 'but don't interrupt.'

'All right, Ruth,' said Notty. He stood up on his shelf and stretched. 'Ruth got a bit cross with me today,' he said comfortably. 'Because I sang a little song in front of some customers.'

Emily and Martha had told Maze about Notty,

but that hadn't prepared her for the reality – first she gaped, then she burst out laughing.

'Isn't he *lovely*?'

'Thank you, Maze,' said the old bear. 'Miss Prizzy has told me all about you – wait till you see her!'

'Don't expect too much.' Ruth lowered her voice. She was holding a shoebox. 'I did what I could – she's pleased, that's the main thing.' She took off the lid of the box. 'Here she is, folks – the new-look Prison Wendy!'

'Ta-*da*!' The ragged doll leapt out in a jumble of bright colours.

If Emily hadn't been on her guard she would have burst out laughing. She had to bite the insides of her cheeks to keep up her serious expression, and she didn't dare look at the others. They couldn't afford to offend the blackmailing toy.

Ruth had done wonders – but Prizzy looked madder than ever.

The red wool plaits had gone; she now had a whole new head of dark purple hair, very cleverly stitched on in cornrows. Her holes had been neatly patched and her gaping seams mended. Ruth had made her a pretty little orange dress. The face had obviously been more of a problem – although Ruth had touched it up with felt tip, nothing could make that huge, wonky grin any less barmy.

'Prizzy, you're *beautiful*!' declared Maze. 'Isn't she?'

'Oh, yes ...' Martha said hastily. 'So ... so ... fashionable.'

'Elegant,' said Emily. 'Ruth, this is brilliant!'

Everyone gave up trying not to laugh. It was impossible not to laugh when Prizzy was proudly walking up and down on the counter, showing off her new dress.

'None of you have mentioned them yet.' Prizzy held up one of her legs. '*Look at my boots!*'

Ruth had made the all-important boots from the stretchy gold material that Martha had rescued from a box of jumble. Prizzy's legs were shaped like stumpy little sausages and the boots were more like socks, but Prizzy loved them. She began to dance, not caring that everyone was now practically crying with laughter.

'We've met all your demands,' Ruth said, once they had all calmed down. 'Now tell us about that broken door.'

'Oh, that!' said Prizzy carelessly. 'We can't mend it now.'

'What? But you promised!'

'The black toad jumped on it and made a great big hole.' Prizzy gazed at her new boots. 'It isn't a secret any more and anyone can get out of Smockeroon for a bit of hard air. Only the Sturvey can fix it and he's *gone*.'

'We should never have trusted you,' Maze said crossly.

A sharp, high, sweet voice said, 'So you're Maze! Your doll has told me so much about you!'

Suddenly, without anyone seeing how it happened, two Barbie dolls had appeared on the shop counter. One was Sister Pretty, in her black nun clothes. And the other—

'Sister Toop!' Emily took a few moments to recognise her.

'Hi, Emily.' The unfairly beautiful Sister Toop was no longer dressed as a nun. Her lovely mass of hair was loose; she was magnificent in a ball gown of rich purple satin. 'It's just Toop now, if you don't mind. I've stopped being a nun. I only did it to keep Pretty company.'

'I've forgiven her,' Sister Pretty explained, rather stiffly. 'It's not her fault she's still in her box. I see that now.'

'I don't have to wear the bag any more, do I?'

'No, dear,' said Sister Pretty. 'The bag is a thing of the past. Thanks to Pippa's inspiring TV broadcasts, I see that I was silly to be jealous. It's quite different now that we can talk back to humans.' She added, with a gracious bow to Ruth, 'We just dropped in to give you our order.'

'Sorry – your order?'

'For gold boots, of course!' said Sister Pretty. 'Thirty-eight pairs – that's for me, Toop and everybody in my Barbie Zumba class. I'll pick them up tomorrow.'

The two Barbies vanished.

'Oh my g— Was that real?' Maze stared at the empty space, blinking like a sleepwalker.

'I'm not making thirty-eight pairs of gold boots,' Ruth said. 'This is an antique shop, not a boot factory.'

'Tell her to buy them at Smartweed's,' said Notty.

'That's the toys' department store,' Ruth said quickly, seeing Maze's bafflement. 'Danny and I made it up after a visit to Selfridges.'

'Wow!' Maze's face was radiant. 'This is incredible – I'm talking to toys! Thanks so much for giving Prizzy a makeover. It must've taken you hours!'

'I'm glad you like the result,' said Ruth, smiling at Maze. 'The hair took longest. And I had to put up with a running commentary while I was working – that stubborn little doll of yours argued over every stitch!'

'She looks wonderful. I was going to say good as new, but I don't remember what she looked like when she was new. Prizzy, say thank you.'

'Bum!' said Prison Wendy. She flicked up her new skirt and rudely flashed her ragged bottom.

Emily and Martha snorted with laughter.

Maze, however, kept her face stern. 'Stop being naughty – there's still space on that top shelf for a prison!'

'*No!*' Prizzy stamped one of her golden feet. 'I'll escape!'

'Say thank you to Ruth.'

'Oh, all right – keep your label on!' Prizzy said sulkily. 'Thanksformygoldboots. Satisfied?'

'You still know how to talk to her,' said Martha. 'And she still listens.'

Emily's phone bleeped; it was a text from Mum, summoning the three girls for tea and lemon drizzle cake.

'You'd better leave Prizzy with me,' Ruth said. 'Something's changed in Smockeroon and I don't trust her in front of your mother. I'll stuff her in my handbag and she can come with me to my Weight Watcher's class.'

★

Later, much later, after Martha and Maze had gone home and supper had been eaten, Emily's phone bleeped again.

It was a text from Ruth, who hated texting. OUTSIDE – COME ALONE.

Mum and Dad were watching television in the sitting room. Emily crept out of the house and Ruth was waiting at the front gate.

'Look at me,' said Ruth breathlessly. 'I mean, just look at me!'

By the dingy light of the streetlamp, Emily saw that Ruth was covered with big blobs of red gloop.

'Jelly,' Ruth said. 'I went to Weight Watcher's and we had a jelly fight!'

'What – everyone?'

'Yes!' A large blob of jelly fell off Ruth's head and

onto the path. 'This is bad, Emily; this is very bad indeed. That door must be fixed *at once*.'

'But not before I've seen Bluey!' Emily protested. 'It can't be fixed until I've seen him!'

'Sorry, we can't afford to wait any longer.'

'Don't you want to see Danny?'

'Only if he's happy,' Ruth said firmly. 'I'd give up wanting to see him if I knew Smockeroon was a happy place again. We've got to find that Sturvey!'

Twenty-one

THE PENGUIN
SOCIETY OUTING

H *ow do we find an old magic bear?*
Christmas was coming, and the window
of Bottleton's only department store was filled with
a display of brand-new bears – bright and glossy
and empty, waiting to be imagined. These vacant
cushions could not have been less like the Sturvey,
which only underlined the general sadness of the first
Christmas without Holly.

This time last year, Emily had made a tiny
cardboard crown for Bluey, painted gold, with
jewels made of fruit gums. Holly couldn't see the
royal Bluey in his crown, but Emily had gently
guided her fingers to feel him, and she had huffed
with delight.

We always opened Bluey's present first.

What would they do this year? How would they bear it?

Her granny normally came for lunch on Christmas Day, along with Mum's sister.

This year granny was going to a friend's house, and Auntie Becky was off to Goa.

Mum was upset about this. 'They're running away from me. They know how hard it is and they can't face it.'

'Look on the bright side,' said Dad. 'It'll be far less work without them. I rather fancy a Christmas where I don't have to listen to my mother complaining about everything. And I certainly won't miss Becky's boxes of horrible vegan food.'

'But it'll be so quiet,' Mum said sadly. 'Just the three of us.'

And the empty space where Holly used to be.

'It's going to be the worst Christmas ever,' Emily told Ruth, when they were alone in the shop. 'I wish I could fall into a deep sleep and wake up when it's over.'

'The first Christmas is a killer,' Ruth said. 'You just have to make up your mind to get through it – if you don't expect it to be fun, you appreciate any nice things that happen all the more.'

'What did you do after Danny died?'

'To be horribly frank with you, that Christmas was one of the times I wanted to die. The whole thing was meaningless without him – I cried for a solid hour when I put up the tree, because there weren't any presents for my Danny to put underneath it.' Ruth sniffed briskly. 'Oh, that black toad had a field day with me! I went off to stay with my brother and his family, but I felt like the loneliest person in the universe.'

There's three of us – but she was left all alone.

'That's awful,' said Emily.

'It got a lot better when the pipes burst,' Ruth said. 'They couldn't find a plumber on Christmas Day, so my brother and I had to climb into the loft to plug up the hole – and it was just the thing to take my mind off black toads. My brother got his bum stuck in a cardboard box and then I nearly died laughing. He's even fatter than I am.'

'Ah – Ruth and Emily!' All of a sudden there was a small, bossy penguin on the counter. 'Just the people I was looking for.' Hugo was carrying a clipboard and wearing what seemed to be a dustpan and brush made of purple velvet on his head. 'I'm collecting names for the outing.'

'Hugo!' Emily was so happy to see him that she almost cried. Ruth thought it was a good sign when they heard nothing from the toys, but she hated it.

'How nice to see you!' Ruth gave him a friendly pat. 'Have you finished rebuilding your top floor?'

'Oh, yes,' said Hugo. 'And it's better than the old one, so I forgave Pippa when she owned up to stealing it.'

'Love the hat,' said Emily. 'Is there any more news about the Sturvey?'

'No, he's still missing. It's very awkward. He's stopped fixing the weather, and now it's too warm and our chocolate money keeps melting. There was a big bank robbery yesterday, but it was easy to catch the criminals – they left so many chocolate footprints.'

'Toy bank robbers!' Emily was alarmed. 'That's impossible!'

'Not any more,' said Hugo with a sad expression that looked completely wrong on his silly face. 'Things are getting really bad in Pointed End. Some mean plastic dinosaurs stole our slide this morning – with poor old Smiffy still on it!' He sighed and looked at his clipboard. 'Now, are you coming?'

'Sorry – coming where?'

'Of course,' said Ruth, 'I'd nearly forgotten – next Wednesday is the Penguin Society's annual outing! Where are you going this year, Hugo?'

'It's a mystery tour,' said Hugo. 'That means it'll be a big surprise when we get there. And I still have a few places on the coach left over for non-penguins.'

Ruth caressed his important little head. 'I'd love to come, but I have to work.'

'And I'll be on a school trip,' said Emily. 'We're going on a tour of Norton's.'

★

The pie factory was the biggest employer in Bottleton and nine girls in Emily's class had parents who worked there. It was a vast place, with as many buildings as a small town. Emily had been here before, but only to the dull grey office block where they kept the accountants.

'They're launching a new pie,' said Amber Jones, whose mother worked in the publicity office. 'Apple with caramel.'

'Sounds good,' said Martha. 'I hope they let us taste it.' They were on the coach and she was next to

Emily. She nudged her and whispered, 'I left Pippa at home – what about Prizzy?'

'Ruth's got her,' Emily whispered back. 'And Maze made her promise not to cause trouble.'

Maze was just across the aisle of the coach, next to Summer, pretending to ignore Emily – they had all agreed about this, because Summer was getting suspicious, and she was the sort of person who made it impossible to talk about babyish stuff like toys.

Emily was on the alert for any sign of silliness at Norton's, such as the throwing pies her dad had rambled about when under the influence of the glitter. So far, everything looked normal; maybe he'd been an isolated case and the infection hadn't spread.

The coach stopped outside a huge grey hangar.

'QUIET!' Mrs Lewis, whose husband did something important at the factory, was in charge today. 'Let me remind you all that while you're wearing your Harriet Cattermole uniforms, you are ambassadors for the school and I expect you to be on your best behaviour!'

She led the girls into the Publicity Suite, a large office with sofas, potted plants and historical pictures of the factory. There was a strong smell of toffee apples.

'Mmmm!' Martha sighed. 'It's making my stomach rumble and we've only just had lunch!'

'The whole place reeks of sugar,' Summer muttered. 'I think it's gross.'

'Hi, everyone. Welcome to Norton's.' A youngish woman in a smart red suit had appeared. 'My name is Clare and I'll be taking you round the factory this afternoon. You'll experience the whole life cycle of our newest apple pie – yes, doesn't it smell wonderful? A couple of facts first: the firm was founded way back in 1876, when a young Bottleton baker named Joseph Norton . . .'

It wasn't exactly boring, but the ordinariness of everything made Emily a lot less anxious and she relaxed enough to pay attention.

First they were all given white coats, white hats and little blue plastic bags to put over their shoes. They saw the raw apples being peeled and cored, and cooked in a metal vat as big as Emily's house. They saw the great machine that dropped perfect circles of pastry onto a conveyor belt, and another machine that wrapped each finished pie in plastic.

'And now, the final stage in the process,' said Clare. 'The tasting!'

Emily's feet had started to ache, and the toffee-apple fumes were making her light-headed. 'No sign of trouble, anyway,' she whispered to Martha.

'I wouldn't be so sure about that,' Martha whispered back. 'Look!'

She pointed up at a single red balloon, gently floating in the warm, sweet air above them.

Nobody else took the slightest bit of notice, though a bright red balloon was not what you expected to see in a pie factory.

And then a well-known voice honked, 'Keep together, everybody! No stragglers!'

Suddenly, there was Hugo, leading a long line of other stuffed penguins across the factory floor, plus a few non-penguins, including Smiffy, Sister Pretty and Toop. All the toys were dressed in white coats and hats. Sister Pretty was helping Smiffy to push a big basket on wheels.

'Whose balloon is that?' snapped Hugo. 'I'd like to remind you all that while we're in this factory, we are ambassadors for the Penguin Society – I expect your best behaviour!'

'Emily, please tell me you can see them and you haven't gone goofy!' Martha gabbled into her ear. 'Please tell me I'm not the only one!'

'Don't worry,' Emily said, 'I can see them, clear as day.'

'Look at the others – what's happened to them?'

Everyone else looked like smiling dummies in a shop window; Mrs Lewis had a broad grin that took years off her. The stench of toffee apple grew more powerful. Humans and toys ignored each other completely (Emily had noticed that the toys often failed to notice things until they were pointed out).

'This has been a fascinating outing,' declared Sister Pretty. 'I had no idea that this famous pie factory was started by two enterprising bears and a plastic horse!'

'That's enough history!' someone called from the crowd. 'When can we have our picnic?'

Martha whispered, 'Is that the puffin from the bookshop? Wow.'

'Shut up – we're sticking to the timetable,' Hugo said firmly. 'The picnic comes *after* the pie fight.'

'Quite right,' said Sister Pretty. 'With all pies included in the price.'

'As many as you can hurl,' added Smiffy.

'Oh, *wow!*' Martha shook with laughter. 'This'll look good when we write our reports!'

Emily was laughing too, though her head felt pleasantly distant and foggy. In a nice, non-painful part of her memory she suddenly saw Holly's face, shining with laughter.

The pie fight was your favourite story ever.

Bluey made the national final and totally thrashed Lord Dogger.

I blew raspberries on your arm – SPLAT!

'Well, we're at the end of the tour now,' Clare told the crowd of oblivious humans. 'It's time for you to sample our latest product for yourselves.'

There was a puff of smoke, and a new sign suddenly appeared on the door behind her: THROWING ROOM.

'I love it!' Martha scrabbled under the white coat to dig her phone out of her pocket (they had been told to leave their phones behind with their bags, but Martha's phone was her main birthday present and she couldn't bear to be parted from it). She began to take pictures. 'I hope they come out – are you OK?'

'I'm fine,' said Emily automatically.

'It's just that your lips have gone a funny colour. Are mine a funny colour?'

The door opened onto a large, bright room, furnished with three long tables. Each table was heaped with strangely cartoonish pies. How big was this place, anyway? Emily blinked and the tables and pies shrank to the height of the toys – who surged towards them with honks of joy.

'TAKE THAT!' shouted Toop, and a pie flew across the room into Hugo's face.

The throwing room turned into a storm of magic glitter as the toys flung pies at each other. They thought it was very funny to get hit, and took hilarious selfies of their splattered faces.

And then a real, human pie landed in Emily's face with a cold, wet 'SPLAT' that left her gasping.

'Ha-ha – gotcha!' yelled Mrs Lewis.

Mrs Lewis?

Before she knew what she was doing, Emily found herself grabbing the nearest pie (chocolate custard) and flinging it right back.

There were pies flying in every direction now, until toys and humans were dripping with blobs of jam, custard and meringue. It was extremely weird – and at first it was huge fun. None of the Hatty Catty girls could resist this golden opportunity to throw a pie at the school's scariest teacher, and Mrs Lewis gave as good as she got, chucking her pies with the precision of a machine.

But then – suddenly – everything was different. It seemed to Emily that in the space of one blink, the pie fight stopped being fun. The silly, furry faces of the toys were scowling and nasty; the laughter turned into shrieks of fury, the pies turned into weapons.

'BUM to you!' the puffin from the bookshop yelled, rubbing Hugo's beak into a chocolate flan. 'You LABEL!'

'OW – STOPPIT!' screamed Sister Pretty. 'Let me go!'

Three girl penguins had surrounded the Barbie nun, and were taking turns to flip up the long skirts of her habit – the mean expressions on their faces made Emily feel sick.

One of them shouted, 'Let's see your SCRIBBLES, plastic lady!' and – to Emily's horror – she ripped off Sister Pretty's veil, exposing the terrible scars on her forehead. 'Hahaha – it says BUM – hahaha!'

'Stop! Stop fighting!' Emily tried to shout, but it

came out as a croak. The horrible sight had stunned her like a blow and her head was reeling. 'You can't hurt each other – you're *toys*!'

'Give it back!' Sister Pretty started to cry – and a crying toy was the worst sight of all.

'Leave her alone!' Emily gasped. 'Hugo, you've got to find Bluey!' One clear thought suddenly rose up in her scrambled mind – Bluey was in the very deepest part of Smockeroon, and the toad hadn't got that far (not yet, anyway). 'He'll help us, I know he will!'

For one fraction of a second, she glimpsed it – the black toad, its eyes slits of pure spite, looming out of the doorway like a storm cloud . . .

Twenty-two

A MEETING
IN WONDERLAND

'SIT DOWN . . . DEEP BREATHS . . . drink this . . .'
Drink Me.

Emily tried to explain that she didn't want to shrink like Alice, but her mouth wouldn't make the words.

Mrs Lewis threw a cold, wet pie into her face.

No – it was a wet wipe.

The hard world rushed back and Emily found herself sitting on one of the sofas in the Publicity Suite, with a bottle of water being held to her lips and an amphitheatre of faces staring down at her.

'You turned a bit faint,' said Mrs Lewis. 'Well, it has been a long afternoon, and you look a lot better now – but I'll tell your mother to take you to the doctor's, just to be on the safe side.'

251

The embarrassment was colossal. Emily's cheeks were on fire. 'I'm fine – honestly . . .'

Did any of that really happen?

She was still stunned by what she had seen, and everyone else seemed slightly stunned too, as if they sensed something important had gone wrong, though they remembered nothing at all about the magic.

'On the coach, everybody!' Mrs Lewis turned her attention back to the other girls, and the terrible staring stopped when Clare started to hand out gift bags that contained small, plastic-wrapped samples of the latest pie.

'Are you really OK?' Martha whispered anxiously. 'Do you swear?'

'I'm fine now. I don't know what happened.'

'Your face went all weird and you nearly fell over – it was quite scary.'

'You saw them, didn't you?'

'Yes, if you mean the toys,' said Martha. 'I can't believe nobody else noticed – they all think we've been on a normal school trip.'

They took their seats on the coach and there was a storm of chatter and pie sampling, which meant they could talk normally, without having to whisper.

'How much did you see?'

'Yum, this pie's fabulous,' said Martha, through a mouthful of sweet pastry. 'You should open yours.'

'You take it.' Emily never wanted to see a pie again in her life. 'Did you see the fight?'

'What fight?'

'There was an enormous pie fight – humans as well as toys. Everyone got covered with custard.'

Martha looked at her uneasily. 'Are you sure you're OK?'

'Yes!'

'I think that part might have been a dream. The toys disappeared when we went into the tasting room. That's when you turned green and keeled over.'

'You were taking photos,' said Emily. 'I'm sure I saw you doing it during the fight.'

'Photos?' Martha pulled her phone from the pocket of her blazer and began to search through the pictures. 'Hey – look! I *did* take photos – but where're they going?'

The pictures that she did not remember taking flashed across the screen and faded into nothing – but not before the two girls had seen them.

The red balloon, the line of penguins, the door that

said 'Throwing Room'. And one startling close-up of the bookshop puffin, snarling as he attacked Hugo.

'His face!' Martha was bewildered and starting to be frightened. 'And that puffin always seemed so friendly. I've known him for years and I still give him a pat when I'm in the bookshop. I don't understand – are all our toys going to turn nasty?'

'I've told Hugo to ask Bluey for help,' said Emily.

'What can he do?'

Emily didn't want to admit that she didn't know. 'He'll think of something.'

★

The end of the stethoscope was cold on Emily's chest and back. It was the next morning, and Mum had insisted on dragging her to the doctor's.

'Nothing the matter here,' Dr Brewer said cheerfully. 'You were quite right to bring her in, but she's as fit as a fiddle. I'm prepared to bet it was nothing more than being tired and dehydrated.' He smiled at Emily. 'You can put your shirt back on – and you've earned a boiled sweet.'

'Thanks.' Emily had known Dr Brewer since she

was a baby, and she liked him; he had grey hair and a baggy old tweed jacket, and he always gave you a piece of barley sugar.

'It's never happened before,' her mother said quietly. 'She hasn't been eating very much since ... well—'

'Mum!' (*Please don't embarrass me!*)

'I worry that she doesn't seem to have grown since we lost Holly.'

'Nonsense!' Dr Brewer said happily. 'People grow at different rates – I'll only worry if that blazer still fits in a year's time.'

Emily said, as patiently as she could manage, 'I really am fine. Honestly.'

'Of course, of course – you're missing that sister of yours.' He looked over her head at Mum. 'Loss of appetite, being quiet and withdrawn – all quite normal in a case like this. Don't expect her to bounce back all at once.'

It was nearly ten o'clock by the time they walked out of the surgery. Mum had phoned the school and the office where she worked to say they would be late; she had refused to listen to Emily saying, again and again, that she was perfectly healthy, and now the whole day was out of shape.

'For the last time,' Mum said wearily, unlocking the car, 'I promised that bossy teacher of yours that I'd have you checked out.'

'Mrs Lewis was exaggerating. I didn't faint at the pie factory – I just felt a bit woozy.'

'Emily, do change the record!' Mum sighed. 'I needed to put my own mind at rest – OK?'

'I told you there was nothing to worry about. Now I'll have to walk in right in the middle of geography, and Ms Khan's really strict.'

'Well, I'm sure she'll understand when you explain.'

This was a very parent-ish thing to say; parents didn't understand that teachers never listened to explanations. Emily gave up the argument. Now that she had got over the worst of the embarrassment and disruption, she felt mean for making her mother anxious.

Mum said, 'Gwen was absolutely lovely about it.' Gwen was her boss. 'And she's already said I can leave early next Wednesday.'

'What's happening next Wednesday?'

'I had a letter from the charity that got us Holly's bed. They're coming to take it away.'

'Oh.'

Holly's specially adapted hospital bed took up most of the space in her room – the last place in the world where a sense of her still lingered. With the bed it was still recognisably Holly's room. When the bed was gone, it would be nobody's room.

'It's silly of me to mind about it,' Mum said sadly. 'I suppose I knew they'd want it back eventually – those beds are terribly expensive. But it'll look so empty.'

'I'm glad you warned me.'

'Of course I warned you,' her mother said. 'You don't need any more sudden changes in your life.'

This was the closest she would come to talking about the morning when Emily had woken up to a life without Holly, the greatest change of all.

I never said goodbye.

This thought was agony. Emily tried to push it away, but it had a way of leaping out to torment her whenever her guard was down.

I didn't kiss you.

I didn't hug Bluey.

I didn't know it would be the last time.

★

'I can't believe I didn't see anything.' Maze's voice was muffled; she was in the middle of pulling her grey school jersey over her head. 'Not a *thing*! All I got was a rather boring tour of a factory and a free pie. Why was I left out?'

'Maybe because you were standing too close to Summer,' suggested Martha 'She's always saying stories about magic are stupid. Maybe it rubbed off.'

'And *who knew* about the puffin from the bookshop? I *liked* that puffin!'

'Don't blame him,' said Emily. 'He was under the influence of the toad.'

'Well, it's not fair. I'm the owner of Prizzy. That ought to count for something.'

'I didn't see everything,' said Martha. 'Emily got most of it.'

'So let me get this straight. The toys turned mean, and you asked Bluey to help.'

'Yes,' said Emily.

'What can he do?'

'I don't know – I thought the Sturvey might be in his bit of Smockeroon.'

It was after lunch and they were in the classroom, getting ready for the dress rehearsal of *Alice in*

Wonderland. They had to stop talking about Smockeroon when Ms Robinson came over to do Maze's make-up. This was their first time in full costume and make-up, and it was so much fun that Emily pushed her worries about the toys to the back of her mind.

She put on the sky-blue dress and white apron that her mother had made. Ms Robinson combed her hair off her face, fixed it with a blue hairband and curled the ends with electric tongs.

'Emily, you've stepped right out of the book!' Ms Robinson pushed her gently towards the long mirror she had brought in. 'Take a look at your transformation.'

It was startling to see how much she looked like the pictures of Alice in the book, and the classroom was suddenly crowded with famous characters. The long red Tudor dress that Mum had made for the Red Queen looked fabulous, especially when Ms Robinson had painted Maze's face dead white, with big, frowning black eyebrows. Martha looked brilliant too, in her huge, furry white rabbit's ears, and Amber Frost had an amazing caterpillar costume made of green cardboard. The classroom was in chaos, every chair and desk piled with discarded clothes and bits of costume and every girl talking at the top of her voice.

At last, when everyone was ready and more or less quiet, Ms Robinson led them all down the small back staircase and onto the stage. There was real stage lighting today; the wings were thrillingly dark.

'Don't forget to treat this as a real performance!' Ms Robinson called to them from the auditorium. 'If anything goes wrong, just carry on!'

The music started, loud and boisterous, and Emily had to concentrate on not tripping over her feet when she ran out onto the stage with the other girls who were in the opening scene.

Summer Watson stepped forward to read the opening poem, 'All in the Golden Afternoon.'

And then Martha the White Rabbit ran out, looking hilarious in her ears and whiskers, and holding a huge watch made of cardboard.

'I'm late! I'm late!'

This was the part of the story everyone remembered, when Alice chases the White Rabbit and falls down the rabbit hole. Ms Robinson had made a large hole in a piece of cardboard and put a black curtain behind it, so that Martha and then Emily would look as if they were being swallowed into the darkness.

Martha climbed through the hole and Emily went in after her, exactly as they had rehearsed.

And this was when Emily noticed something was different. She was supposed to run back onto the stage as soon as she heard the swirling, electronic music that Ms Robinson had written for Alice's endless fall down the rabbit hole. When all the noises of the play suddenly went silent, she thought at first that the sound system had gone wrong, and turned to say something to Martha.

But everyone backstage, including Martha and the crowd of animals waiting to run on for the Caucus Race, was strangely still and quiet, like people in a stopped film.

And then she saw a pale light glowing around the nearby fire extinguisher, and a huddle of small shapes on the floor.

'Hello, Emily!' It was Hugo, looking very pleased with himself. 'Sorry to interrupt – it won't take long.'

'Hugo, what're you doing here?'

'Bluey's sent you a message.'

'Bluey?' Pain and joy whipped through her; she'd

been wondering if she'd fainted again, and now she didn't care. 'Is he here?'

'He can't come Hardside any more,' said Hugo. 'And it's a complicated message about the Sturvey, so he turned it into a catchy song and sent his choir – he still keeps it for special occasions.'

The toys around the fire extinguisher shuffled into three tidy rows, with the tallest at the back. They coughed and rustled their sheets of music, and then burst out singing:

> *It starts with an E and Entrance is free!*
> *Then comes number TWO, which rhymes*
>   *with Pooh!*
> *And next is NINE; that's just fine!*
> *Followed by P, in time for tea!*
> *Last comes A, which is a new experience for A*
>   *because A is usually first!*

Emily clapped politely at the end, not wanting to hurt the choir's feelings – but the song sounded like total nonsense.

'That's it,' said Hugo happily. 'He'll send you another message when you get there.'

'Get *where?*'

The toys vanished, the light vanished.

Behind her, Martha giggled and whispered, 'I've lost one of my whiskers!'

It was an ordinary dress rehearsal again.

The electronic music began and Emily ran back on stage without missing a beat. The rest of the performance went perfectly, but the fact that Bluey had answered her cry for help warmed her like a hot-water bottle.

Afterwards, when they were back in the classroom, she pulled Maze and Martha behind the costume rail, to whisper, 'Come back with me – you won't believe what just happened!'

Twenty-three

THE MESSAGE

RUTH WAS INTRIGUED by Bluey's message. She made Emily sing it several times and wrote the words down on a piece of paper. 'Now it makes even less sense! Do you have any idea what it means?'

'No,' said Emily. 'Not a clue.'

'We thought you might know,' said Maze.

Martha glanced up at the shelf, where Notty and Figinda Faraway sat with their steaming mugs of Biggins' Mixture. 'Notty, do you understand it?'

'No,' said Notty. 'I think it must be a secret code. What about you, Figgy?'

'Don't ask me,' said Figinda Faraway. 'I'm far too exhausted. I went shopping at Smartweed's and my money melted all over my dress.'

Ruth said, 'We know this message is important.

Bluey's obviously taken a lot of trouble to get it to us. He even trained his choir to sing it.'

'I don't think it's in code,' said Emily. 'The Bluey I knew wasn't clever enough.'

'A code.' Ruth repeated the word, staring at the nonsensical verse on her piece of paper. 'Well, let's see. What if we take just the letters and numbers in the song? 'It starts with an E, then it's number two.'

She ended up with a short line of numbers and letters – E29PA.

'E29PA,' Emily repeated it. 'What's that supposed to mean?'

'Wait a minute . . .' Ruth's eyes lit up. 'I'm an idiot! I've been writing my Christmas cards all day so I should've seen it at once – it's a postcode!'

'Of course!' Emily was so excited that she could hardly get the words out. 'That means an address! And Hugo said it was something to do with the Sturvey!'

'I'll look it up.' Martha took her phone out of her pocket. Emily and Ruth stood on either side of her, watching the screen impatiently. 'This can't be it – it's just a list of museums.'

'Oh my garters!' Ruth cried out. 'I don't believe it!

How wonderfully appropriate!' She began to shake with laughter. 'E2 9PA is the postcode of the Museum of Childhood in Bethnal Green – the country's largest collection of toys!'

'So Bluey's sending me to a toy museum.' Emily quickly got over a slight feeling of disappointment that the message had not been about Holly and thought about it properly. 'Of course! It's the obvious place to find an antique bear!'

'And Figinda called the Sturvey the most imagined bear in the world,' said Ruth. 'Now I understand why. Thousands of children have seen him and loved him, and filled him with huge amounts of imagination. And we know that this is the fuel that runs Smockeroon. I wonder what went wrong?'

'There's only one way to find out,' said Emily. 'Bluey wants us to go there.'

'That might be tricky,' Ruth said. 'You lot have school during the week, and I can't afford to leave the shop on a Saturday.'

Martha was looking at her phone again. 'It's open on Sundays.'

'Well, that makes all the difference – I can drive down to London this Sunday, if you can think of something to tell your parents.' There was a moment of breathless silence while they looked at each other's excited faces.

We're going to find the Sturvey!

★

Emily's mother had arranged a visit to Auntie Becky in Wolverhampton on Sunday and was annoyed that Emily flatly refused to give up her trip to London.

'I do wish you'd asked me first.'

'You didn't ask *me*,' Emily pointed out.

Luckily, Dad was on Emily's side. On Sunday morning, when Mum started complaining again, he laughed behind his newspaper, and said, 'What a strange girl you are, Emily – how can you bear to miss all those lovely bean sprouts?' And he gave her some extra money for lunch, cheerfully telling her to spend it on burgers. 'Have a double whopper and fries, and think of me.'

'Thanks, Dad.'

Emily was so excited that the excitement had sunk into her bones and made her oddly calm.

The Sturvey!

She had a strong sense of approaching magic, looming like a wave on the point of breaking, and when they were all gathered in Ruth's kitchen, it was obvious the others felt it too; Martha was far less giggly than usual, and Maze kept singing, 'We're *off* to see the Sturvey . . .'

'Right, before we set off,' said Ruth, 'let's do a final check – is everyone here?'

She wasn't talking about humans; they had decided to take certain toys with them, partly to attract the maximum amount of magic, and partly in case they were needed to communicate with Bluey.

Very seriously, they checked their bags. Martha had brought Pippa, Maze had Prizzy and Ruth's large backpack contained Hugo and Smiffy.

'Just a bunch of soft toys at the moment.' Maze was disappointed. 'Can't they feel the magic?'

'We don't need them yet,' said Martha. 'They're saving their strength. I know something's going to happen.'

Ruth zipped up her son's old toys. 'Let's hope they don't go off while I'm driving. We'd better keep them zipped until we get there.'

Twenty-four

SHOWDOWN

THEY ARRIVED AT the museum in the early afternoon, after a hasty hamburger lunch on the motorway.

'Well, here we are,' said Ruth.

The museum was warm, bright and welcoming, and crowded with families. Emily looked around at the children, the parents with buggies and the smiling museum staff – where was Bluey's 'message'?

'The toys might know – our toys, I mean.' Martha shrugged off her backpack and unzipped the pocket where she kept Pippa.

They all stared silently at the very unmagic stuffed toy.

Maze asked, 'So what do we do now?'

'I'm not sure,' said Emily. 'But we know we're searching for an old bear.'

Ruth groaned softly. 'Talk about finding a needle in a haystack – this place is absolutely crowded with old bears! It must be the highest concentration of old bears in the Western world.'

'We'll have to look at all of them, that's all. It won't take that long if we walk quickly. Bluey wouldn't drag us all this way without leaving a clue – he promised.' Emily went over to the large floor plan on one wall that showed the various galleries in the museum. 'And we don't need to go round the whole place. Lots of these rooms are just Meccano, or train sets.'

'Good thinking!' Ruth recovered her briskness and put on her glasses to study the floor plan. 'Let's see – Lego, doll's houses, toy cars, antique babyclothes . . . Ah, this is more like it – teddy bears and soft toys.'

'We'll know the sign when we see it,' said Emily, with a confidence she did not feel. 'Come on.'

They set off very seriously, like a group of explorers. As Ruth had said, there was no shortage of old bears in this famous museum – but not a single scrap of magic. Emily pressed her face against each glass case she passed, with increasing desperation. These ancient toys, with their wise, worn little faces, stayed stubbornly toyish. Though nobody said anything, Maze had begun to be restless, and Martha kept glancing hopefully at signs for the cafe.

Emily's backpack was getting heavier. She listened with half an ear to the tish-tish-tish sound of someone's radio.

'Honestly, some people!' Ruth muttered crossly. 'You'd think they'd have the courtesy to switch off that noise pollution!'

The sound got louder.

> *. . . a kind friend told me what to do –*
> *He said BEARCORF is the thing for you!*

'That's a toys' advert!' Emily cried out joyfully. 'Where's it coming from?'

They all listened to the distant babble of music and voices.

'*. . . this is Radio Smockeroon . . . MORE sunny weather . . . a good idea to put your chocolate money in the fridge . . .*'

It faded into silence.

'Well, that's got to be some sort of sign,' said Ruth.

'Emily – your *bag*!' Maze blurted out suddenly. 'Look!'

'It's like my sleepover!' said Martha.

When she took off her bag, Emily saw that white light was streaming out of the pocket where she kept the Bluey book, bright enough to make them all screw up their eyes.

The pink notebook was warm when Emily's fingers closed around it, and the light dwindled to a soft neon glow. But there was something else – a scrap of paper had suddenly appeared stuck to one of the glass cases, with an arrow drawn in purple crayon.

'Bluey!' Emily was so fiercely happy, and so proud of Holly's chief toy that she had to blink away a few tears. 'I knew he wouldn't let us down.'

'I owe that bear an apology,' said Ruth. 'We should have guessed he'd use your notebook to send his messages – it's all about him, after all.'

'Nobody's looking at us.' Maze glanced at the other people strolling through the gallery.

Emily followed the direction of the arrow and saw another sign – IN HERE – this time stuck to a blank door that said NO ENTRY – STAFF ONLY.

Ruth tried to open the door. 'It's locked!' She

rattled the handle impatiently. 'Could you ask Bluey to find a key?'

Emily tried, and the door opened perfectly.

'You're obviously in charge,' said Maze, grinning. 'Now's your chance to show some leadership.'

'Fine by me.' Ruth took a step back. 'You go first – quick, before someone notices.'

'OK.' The idea of being in charge would normally have made Emily nervous and clumsy, afraid of doing something wrong; now she was totally confident.

I'm getting messages from Bluey.

She led them through the door, which took them into a dull corridor lined with offices, eerily quiet after the bustle of the museum.

'Nobody's going to stop us,' said Maze. 'There's nobody here.'

'Let's hope we don't set off any alarms,' said Martha.

The next note appeared on a door at the far end of the corridor – IN HERE.

This door had a keypad and Emily did not know the code, but it opened as soon as she touched the handle.

On the other side of the door, they found themselves in a stone stairwell that looked much older than the rest of the building – dark and dusty, with feeble strip lighting and antique fire extinguishers on the landings. There was a deep, deep silence.

Maze asked, 'Is this still the museum?'

'It looks like nobody's been here for years,' said Martha, brushing a cobweb off her sleeve. 'So, where to now?'

The pink notebook was warm in Emily's hand. No new message had appeared, but she knew where to go next. Moving more slowly now, she led them down two flights of stairs, through a pair of swing doors, and into a long, deserted passageway.

Emily was tingling all over with the feeling she thought of as 'Blueyness' – the feeling she'd had when she told one of her stories to Holly. It had never felt like making something up; more like slipping into a special state of mind. 'Look!' She grabbed Maze's arm. 'Look at that sign!'

A wooden sign, badly written and covered with cobwebs, hung from the ceiling.

STURVEY THIS WAY.

They all felt the Blueyness now, and stared at the sign in breathless silence.

'Wow, we really are off to see the Sturvey – this is

just like *The Wizard of Oz*!' Ruth let out a nervous giggle. 'I think we can assume we're not in Kansas any more!'

A few yards later, another sign appeared.

BOW OR CURTSEY HERE.

Emily bowed low, like a prince in a cartoon fairy tale, and Maze and Martha burst into nervous giggles.

'Come on – for all we know, we're being watched.' Ruth dropped an elaborate curtsey. 'Just obey the sign!'

Martha and Maze bowed, and stopped giggling.

The long, dusty, deserted corridor finally ended at a single door.

Maze read the faded hard-world sign aloud. 'Long-term storage.'

'I thought Bluey was taking us to the Sturvey.' Emily was fiercely disappointed. The magic had suddenly been ripped away. 'This is just some old stockroom.'

'We can't give up now,' said Martha. 'Open the door.'

Emily touched the door. It swung open, slowly and creakily.

Inside the room everything was stillness and

silence, faintly lit by a strip light on the ceiling. The room was large and long, with deep shelves that were crowded with cardboard boxes and plastic bags. Each box or bag had a neat label: 'MATCHBOX SPORTS CARS 1950s', 'DIE-CAST FARMYARD SETS 1930s', 'SMALL STEIFF BEARS 1970s'.

Beyond the shelves was a group of glass cases, all standing about at odd angles, like people at a party. The glass cases were in shadow. Emily saw the black outlines of the antique toys that had once been on display in the Museum upstairs.

'Poor old things,' said Ruth softly. 'Shoved in here and forgotten, as if they'd never been played with.'

'Shhh – I can hear something!' Martha hissed suddenly. 'What's that noise?'

They listened, and out of the silence came a wheezing, huffing sound, as regular as Holly's breathing machine.

Arf-arf-arf-arf.

'It sounds like Podge,' said Ruth. 'Cat snores.'

The sound got louder, and they all jumped when a light suddenly came on in the glass case next to Emily. It contained one very old bear.

Emily read out the card beside it. 'Bear, Hummel

Factory, Leipzig 1902. Donated to the Museum by . . .
S. Turvey.'

The name hung on the air.

S. Turvey!

'Wow – we've done it!' Emily said softly. 'We've
found the Sturvey!'

Thank you, Bluey.

The excitement was intense and incredible. They
were standing before the most imagined bear in
the world.

A handsome brown bear, with a long snout and a
humped back.

Where had they seen him before?

Emily and Ruth remembered at the same moment,
and cried out together: 'It's the German lodger!'

Twenty-five

A VERY IMPORTANT JOB

THE ANCIENT TOY SHIFTED on his Perspex stand. 'Too hard!' he muttered. 'My chocolate egg is much too hard!'

'WAKE UP!' shouted Emily. 'Mr Sturvey – or whatever your name is – you've got to save Smockeroon!'

His glass eyes glinted at them. 'Where am I? What's going on? Ach, I tried to tell them – they should never have put me here!'

'WAKE UP!' shouted everyone.

'Oh . . . oh . . . a little strength is creeping back into my stuffing!' The Sturvey's arms quivered feebly. 'But I'm so dreadfully weak – I can do nothing!'

'Maybe he's hungry,' said Martha. 'I wish we had some Biggins' Mixture.'

Ruth said, 'I wish Danny was here. He'd know what to do.'

'And I wish . . .' Emily suddenly felt a great wave of sadness washing over her.

What's the point of silly stories without Holly?

What's the point of anything?

'Eeyew!' Martha clamped a hand over her nose. 'That's disgusting!'

'Yuck – I think I'm going to throw up,' groaned Maze. 'That smells like about a million concentrated farts!'

The stench hit Emily a second later, and the room filled with the desolate sound of countless people sobbing and wailing.

The toad!

It was in the room with them, blocking the door – black and oozing, slowly blinking its wicked eyes.

Maze and Martha screamed.

'Do something!' Emily banged on the Sturvey's case so hard that she nearly broke the glass. 'Get rid of it!'

'I can't.' The old bear sighed. 'They shut me away and I ran out of fuel.'

'What fuel?'

'Human imagination – I can't help Smockeroon without it. You must help me.' He stood up on shaky old legs. 'My strength is coming back, but it's not enough. Join hands!'

Emily grabbed Ruth's hand on one side of her and Martha's on the other. The four of them made a circle around the glass case.

'Think about your toys!' cried the Sturvey. 'Think about them as hard as you can!'

It was difficult to think about anything except the smell, which was getting stronger; knowing how important this was, Emily made a mighty effort to concentrate.

Bluey, Bluey, Bluey, Bluey.

There was a dazzling starburst of colour, and the glass cases suddenly lit up like little theatres, with antique toys moving and murmuring inside them. Many of them were old bears, but there were all kinds of other animals – including a truly ancient group of small stuffed monkeys in red jackets, all with musical instruments, and two moth-eaten lady rabbits in straw hats. The glass melted away and they jumped out of the cases onto the floor. A swarm of small toys began to climb out of their boxes and bags on the shelves.

'More!' cried the Sturvey. 'Think harder!'

Bluey!

Ruth gasped suddenly and clutched Emily's hand tighter. Her backpack heaved violently, the zip burst open, and Hugo and Smiffy jumped out onto the floor.

'WELL DONE, RUTH!' shouted Hugo. 'That was some very hard thinking!'

'Hi, Martha!' The small yellow shape that was Pippa leapt out of Martha's backpack.

'Hi, Maze!' yelled the rough voice of Prizzy, 'HAVE I MISSED THE FIGHT?'

And the floor was suddenly a carpet of toys, shoving and jostling and arguing.

The massed toys bravely bombarded the toad with pies and sweets, until the air was thick with magic glitter. Hugo and Smiffy charged towards it, flourishing a weapon that looked like a vacuum cleaner – until Emily saw that the nozzle was squirting out a powerful jet of something sweet and gloopy.

'A turbotrifle!' gasped Ruth. 'For a toy, that's the equivalent of a rocket-launcher! But why isn't it working?'

The black toad was swelling and growing before their despairing eyes.

'I'M NOT SCARED OF YOU!' shouted Hugo furiously. 'Danny says you're just FAT and STUPID – so there!'

The toad suddenly lashed out a long black rope of a tongue and pulled the stuffed penguin into its revolting mouth, until only his furry feet were sticking out.

'Hugo!' Ruth was nearly crying. 'Oh, please – please give him back!'

Emily wasn't scared now, or sad, but furiously angry. Before she properly knew what she was doing, she marched across the floor, grabbed Hugo's feet and heaved him out of the toad's mouth. 'I don't care what you do to me – leave the toys alone!'

She gave Hugo to Ruth, who hugged him hard.

Hugo's beak opened and shut, but no sound came out; for once, the talkative penguin was lost for words.

'Thanks, Emily,' said Ruth. 'I can't live without . . . I can't . . .' She sniffed a couple of times, then turned to face the toad.

'You've been tormenting me since I lost Danny, but I refuse to let you spoil the one happy place I had left – get out! You don't belong in Smockeroon, or the Land of Neverendings – or whatever we decide to call it!'

'Not enough!' moaned the Sturvey.

'Well, what else are we supposed to do?' Ruth snapped.

'Throw something at it!' the old bear cried. 'Some really *hard* imagination!'

'What on earth are you talking about?'

Emily suddenly had an idea. She shrugged off her backpack, unzipped the secret pocket and pulled out the Bluey book. This was packed with imagination.

I've poured in so much, there's only one blank page left.

She threw the Bluey book at the black toad, as hard as she could.

It hit the toad right between the eyes.

There was an extraordinary sound – a loud explosion, mixed with a wet squelch like a wellington boot being pulled out of deep mud.

And then silence.

The closed gallery was dark again; the museum toys were still and silent in their glass cases.

Nobody spoke. The four humans stared at each other, and the silence stretched on.

'Your notebook!' whispered Maze, gaping at the empty space where the black toad had been. 'It's gone!'

Emily thought about this, and found that she didn't mind. 'I don't think I need it now. I only started it because I was scared of forgetting Holly and Bluey – and they were safe in my memory all along.'

'Some things can't be forgotten,' said Ruth. 'Even if you try.'

'Now the Sturvey will be able to answer his messages.' Emily looked at the old German bear in his case. He was a stuffed toy again, but there was something different about him – an extra gleam in his glass eyes, an expression of wisdom stitched into his face.

'He wasn't getting enough human imagination,' Ruth said. 'We know that's what powers the whole of Smockeroon. When the Sturvey was locked away down here, with not a single human to feed him, he lost his power and Smockeroon broke out in total chaos.'

'We should break into the museum once a month,' suggested Maze. 'Just to top him up if it happens again.'

'I don't think that'll be necessary,' said Ruth, very thoughtfully. 'I've had a rather brilliant idea – we can use Blokey, Mokey and Figinda as bargaining chips. OK, they don't really belong to me, but nobody else knows that. I'll offer them to this museum . . . if they agree to put the Sturvey back on display, where he'll be seen by as many children as possible.'

Emily, Martha and Maze looked at each other, thinking about this.

Maze asked, 'But will the Museum agree to it?'

'Trust me,' said Ruth, 'those toys are legendary – when I pretend to "find" them, it'll be a sensation.'

'Is this it, then?' asked Martha. 'Is this the end of all the magic?'

'I think so.' Ruth was smiling, but her eyes were sad. 'I'll miss Hugo and Smiffy.'

'I'll miss Pippa.'

'I suppose I'll miss Prizzy,' said Maze. 'Can we go to the cafe now? I could *murder* a Twix!'

'And I could do serious damage to a piece of cake,' said Martha, breaking out in giggles. 'I hope they have chocolate.'

'I'll settle for a cup of tea,' said Ruth. 'My feet are killing me!' She touched Emily's arm. 'Are you OK?'

'Yes, I'm fine.' Emily kept the feeling to herself, but she couldn't be as happy as the others.

I didn't see Bluey.

★

It was pitch dark when Ruth's big, battered Volvo drew up outside Barkstone Bygones.

The lights were on in the sitting room of Emily's house. She thought how welcoming the glowing windows looked at the end of the long path.

Holly's not there – but it feels like our proper home again.

Her mother came to one of the windows to draw the curtains; she'd been pale and tired for the last couple of weeks, but now she was smiling and saying something to Dad over her shoulder. They must have enjoyed their lunch in Wolverhampton.

I'm coming home to happy people.

'Well, girls,' Ruth said, 'it's been quite an adventure. We found the famous Sturvey, and he's probably mending that broken door as we speak – but there's one more thing we need to do before it shuts forever.'

'What thing?' asked Maze.

286

'I know,' said Emily, looking at Ruth. 'It's your idea for fixing the fuel supply. I hope we're not too late.'

A sudden movement in the shop window made them all jump; it was Notty, waving at them to come inside.

'There's your answer,' said Ruth. 'That door's not quite mended yet – come on.'

They all followed Ruth to her back door and into the shop. She switched on the overhead light and picked up her mother's ancient bear. He was covered with glitter and a pink paper streamer dangled from one of his arms.

'Well done!' said Notty. 'I heard all about it on the radio – I came straight from the party.'

Ruth patted his venerable head. 'I need to speak to Blokey and Mokey and Figinda – can you fetch them?'

'It's a bit awkward now,' said Notty. 'Blokey's in the middle of leading a sing-song.'

'This is really important,' said Emily.

'All right – if you insist.' The disintegrating bear blinked his glass eyes, and a second later they all heard scrabbling sounds from the box under the counter where Ruth kept the three Staples toys. They climbed out, all trailing paper streamers.

'It had better be important!' the tin monkey said

crossly. 'I was just about to propose a toast to Bluey.'
He flashed a friendly grin at Emily. 'You must be very
proud of him.'

'Yes, incredibly proud,' said Emily, with the usual
stab of longing for Holly and her bear. 'His messages
were wonderful.'

'Yes – wonderful!' said Martha.

'Bluey's a total star!' said Maze.

Ruth gazed down at the three small, grubby little
figures on the counter. 'I'm afraid we called you here
to say goodbye.'

'No!' cried Figinda Faraway crossly. 'I don't want
to go back to that smelly old trunk – the hard world
is *brilliant*!'

'Let me finish,' said Ruth. 'You won't be in the trunk.
In the hard world you'll be in your cardboard box right
here – but only until you can start your new job.'

'Job?' Ms Faraway's glass eyes flashed beadily.

'Yes, and I think you're going to love it; you're
going to be in a very posh glass case, where you'll
see *thousands* of humans . . .' Ruth briefly outlined
her plan, and it was good to see the delight that was
dawning on the faces of the three Edwardian toys.

'This is a dream come true,' said Figinda Faraway.

'Though I suppose I'll have to take off this beautiful dress that Pippa lent me.'

'Your rags will get mended once you're in the museum,' said Emily, remembering the immaculate condition of the antique toys they had seen today. 'The experts will clean you up properly, not just with a J-cloth.'

'You're priceless antiques,' said Maze.

The stitched faces of the three toys were very serious, with the beginnings of great excitement.

'I can have treatment for my rust,' said Blokey. 'And a lick of new paint!'

'And I can get my wobbly wheel fixed,' said the wooden donkey.

'It'll be fun to be white again, instead of *grey*!' Figinda stepped daintily out of her pink dress, and was suddenly wearing her rags once more. 'And won't it be nice to see the Sturvey again? I've missed our games of Smockeroon Monopoly.'

'You're going to be famous,' Martha said, smiling but a little sad. 'You'll be on postcards.'

'More than that,' said Ruth. 'When I pretend to discover you all, it'll be a sensation – you'll probably be on the TV news.'

'Wow,' said Maze. 'That'll be so weird.'

The stitches of the Staples toys were now smiling radiantly.

'Won't John be pleased?' beamed Mokey.

'I can't wait to tell him,' said Blokey, creaking his tin tail. 'Of course we'll keep our house in Deep Smockeroon, but I'm looking forward to all the *delicious* imagination we'll get in our new job – especially from children.'

Mokey gave Ruth's hand a friendly flick with his tail. 'Thank you for keeping us in your shop.'

'It was my pleasure,' said Ruth. 'I'll miss you all terribly. It's going to be far too quiet without you.'

'We're leaving you with a thank-you present,' said Figinda Faraway. 'It was going to be for Christmas. I wanted to get you a novelty fart with a pretty tune. Unfortunately that wasn't possible, so we found something for you in the hard world.'

'In your cellar,' said Blokey. 'Look in the bottom drawer of the old filing cabinet.'

'The filing cabinet?' Ruth was puzzled. 'It's full of old gas bills, and buried under about a ton of junk – are you sure?'

'Wait and see!' giggled Figinda Faraway.

'We'll be off now,' said Mokey. 'Best wheel forward!'

Emily was glad the problem of the Staples toys had been solved, but tears sprang to her eyes when she kissed them all goodbye.

'I hope you'll come and see us in the museum,' said Blokey. 'We won't be able to move about like this, of course. You'll have to imagine that we're *trying* to wave and sing to you.'

The three soon-to-be-famous toys jumped off the table and scuttled into the kitchen. The humans dashed after them in time to see them climbing through the cat flap into the dark garden. For one second the tiny figures stood in the cold night air, smiling and waving.

And then they were gone.

Twenty-six

INVITATION TO
A POSH BALL

THE NEXT MORNING was Monday. Emily woke early, and lay in bed thinking about yesterday's adventure. They had found the mysterious Sturvey, who had already started to fix the broken door. The black toad had been driven out of Smockeroon. It was a perfect happy ending – but she couldn't shake off her disappointment that she hadn't seen Bluey.

The magic couldn't stretch that far.

She didn't sense the change until she was eating Weetabix at the kitchen table, listening with half an ear to the news on the radio.

'Finally, the Prime Minister has announced that as part of National Play Week, there will be a series of picnics for children and their toys. She added that children of all ages, from one to a hundred, would be welcome; she has promised to attend the picnic in Hyde Park with her teddy bear, Belinda.'

'That's nice!' Mum turned off the radio. 'The Prime Minister's old bear!'

Was the madness leaking out again? Emily was alarmed – until Dad snorted rudely and said,

'She should ask Belinda to do something about the economy – a stuffed bear can't be any sillier than her cabinet.'

Her parents were perfectly happy, but they did not have the air of dreaminess that had been so disturbing on the night of the book group. And there was nothing particularly strange about the fact that the Prime Minister had an old teddy bear – didn't everyone? People put their old toys in lofts and garages, but they never forgot them or threw them away. So everything was back to normal.

And yet . . .

Maybe it was because she was thinking about toys that Emily kept seeing them. On the way to school, babies' buggies seemed to be festooned with more stuffed animals than usual. They passed a dustbin lorry with a large pink bear fixed to its radiator, and nearly every car seemed to have a small toy dangling behind the mirror.

There was nothing magic about any of this, but Emily had a sense that the awakening of the Sturvey had made toys so happy that the happiness had somehow spread to their owners.

Stuffing-waves.

When Holly was sad, Bluey had sent special invisible stuffing-waves to cheer her up.

Thanks to Bluey, the whole town had been engulfed by a vast stuffing-wave.

She was sure of it when she went into her classroom and saw both Maze and Martha huddled around Summer Watson and staring into her bag.

Maze – very excited and trying not to laugh – grabbed Emily's sleeve to pull her over to Summer's desk.

Summer barely noticed Emily; she was in the middle of describing a row with her mother. 'She was the one who decided I wanted a grown-up bedroom. She just took my toys away and put them in the loft without asking me. So I told her I wanted my things back. She said my toys were just rubbish, so I said, "OK, I want my rubbish back." And I went right up to the loft and found my favourite Barbie from when I was little. I mean, OK, I'd let her get into a bit of a state – but I still like her and she's still *mine*.'

Emily looked inside Summer's backpack, and suddenly understood why Maze and Martha were shaking with suppressed laughter.

Squashed between two textbooks was a battered old Barbie doll. She was naked, her long blonde hair was a scruffy tangle – and she had 'BUM' written across her forehead in blue biro.

Sister Pretty!

Emily managed not to yelp this out loud, but the amazing discovery that the strong-minded toy nun belonged to Summer Watson was yet another sign of the explosion of happiness in Smockeroon.

Emily woke up in the middle of Tuesday night, and her first, muddled thought was that Holly was crying. The end of the sound echoed in her mind – the high, thin wailing sound that Holly had made when she was frightened, or in pain, and nothing would comfort her except Emily stroking her cheek with Bluey's soft paw.

She sat up in bed and switched on the lamp. The house was silent, there was no sign of magic, but she had a sudden impulse to go into Holly's bedroom.

The emptiness was as sad as ever, and when they took away the special bed, the room would look even more desolate. It had once been the beating heart of home, where Holly's face shone out from the pillow and Bluey smiled beside her.

In my stories it was a magic flying bed.

Now it's just a lump of metal.

A single sheet of paper fluttered down from the ceiling. Emily grabbed it eagerly and smiled to see the mad, toyish writing: the door had been closed, but a few last scraps of magic were still getting through.

INVITASHUN!
You R perlitely inViTedd to
A CAUcus race and POsH BALL
This WENsdy afTER Tea
ThE SyCAMores
POInted ENd.

The Caucus Race came from *Alice*, and Emily saw why the toys would enjoy it – a race that nobody won, and at the same time, everybody. She couldn't get to the ball, but was very touched to be invited.

The writing on the paper was fading away while she

looked at it, but there was just enough time to read the line at the bottom of the page before it vanished: 'PS No pane here.'

Of course not. How kind of Hugo to remind her. Wherever in the universe Holly had gone, the one thing Emily knew for certain was that there was no more pain. It was a good thought; she was almost cheerful when she went back to bed.

Twenty-seven

EVERYBODY WINS

WEDNESDAY WAS THE DAY of the final performance of *Alice*; the glamorous evening performance for family and friends. It began like a birthday. Emily came down to a 'Good Luck' card, with a picture of Alice on the front. Inside, Dad had written, 'Break a leg!' (which is what people say to actors, for some reason).

Mum said, 'We'll make sure we get there early, to grab the best seats. Ruth's coming, and Neil and Mandy from the pub.'

'Half the town's coming,' said Dad. 'You'll be performing before the cream of Bottleton society.'

'Stop it – you'll make her nervous.' Mum smiled at Emily. 'All you need to remember is that the audience is full of your friends.'

Emily had been in plays at her old school, but only one of her parents (mostly Dad) had come to see her because Holly couldn't help making her loud noises and someone had to stay at home. This evening, for the very first time, they were both coming, and after the show they were all going out for supper at the pub.

The Caucus Race was the funniest scene in Ms Robinson's version of *Alice in Wonderland*. A group of small animals, led by Amber Jones in a mouse mask, held their silly race which had no rules and no losers; they did a brilliant dance to a song Ms Robinson had written called 'Everybody Wins!' and the applause at the end went on for ages.

Emily tried not to look at her parents and Ruth in the second row, though it was nice to know they were there. She was concentrating on being Alice and knew she was acting better than she had ever done in her life – it was lovely to hear the warm waves of laughter from the audience, in all the right places.

And then the world flipped inside out.

The audience, the stage, the school vanished; there was soft grass under her feet, and warm, golden light around her, soft as velvet. Emily took a deep breath of the sweet air and was filled with happiness.

SMOCKEROON!

She was here at last, dazzled by the colours of the flowers, the deep blue of the sky, the rainbow chaos of toys in their finest clothes.

'Emily! I'm so glad you could come!' honked Hugo. 'I knew the Sturvey could do it!'

'Hi, Hugo!' It took Emily a second to recognise him; the penguin was swamped in a huge suit of yellow and brown stripes with only his beak sticking out. 'What on earth are you wearing?'

'This is my fancy-dress costume for the ball,' said Hugo. 'I'm a bee.'

'A bee? Oh, I can see it now. I like your wings.'

'And I've come as a kind pirate,' said Smiffy. The bobbled old bear was wearing an eyepatch, big gold earrings and a black pirate hat, but the skull-and-crossbones on the hat had a friendly smile. 'The Sturvey said you couldn't come back now he's mended the door. But Bluey said you were a special case and he changed his mind.'

'Is Bluey here? Will I be able to see him?'

Will I see Holly?

300

'Of course he's coming to the ball,' said Hugo. 'Everyone's coming – the whole of Smockeroon is joining the grand celebration.'

'The Sturvey banished the black toad for life,' Smiffy said happily. 'Now nobody's fighting any more and the air doesn't smell of pooh.'

Emily vaguely wondered what was happening in the hard world, on the stage at school. Did the audience think she'd fainted – or died? Had time stopped? She was loving this too much to care. 'I bet you were surprised, when you found out the truth about your German lodger!'

'We certainly were,' said Hugo. 'We always knew he was important – just not *that* important! He's given us the vital job of making sure he doesn't fall asleep again, which is what happens when he runs out of fuel.'

'But what'll you do when Blokey's gone, and you can't tell the time?'

'The Sturvey sent us a new cuckoo,' said Smiffy. 'She's really nice.'

'My dear Emily, welcome to our ball!' A Barbie doll hopped out of the milling crowd of toys around them – a very elegant Barbie with smooth blonde hair, proudly wearing a beautiful ballgown of scarlet satin. 'Don't you know me, dear?'

'Sister Pretty – you look gorgeous!'

'Thank you, dear. As you see, I've stopped being a nun.'

'What happened to your scar?'

'Summer scrubbed off my scribbles last night,' said the former nun. 'The horrid word has totally *gone* – I am once more *fabulous*.'

'HELLO, EMILY!' A jaunty little figure skipped towards her. 'LOOK AT MY HAT!'

'Wow,' said Emily, 'you're a Seam-Rite Girl!'

Prison Wendy's dream had come true at last; her bonkers face beamed with joy. 'Yes! Will you tell Maze for me?'

'Of course – she'll be thrilled.'

The sweeping lawns of The Sycamores were now a seething, wriggling mass of toys.

Hugo blew the whistle around his neck until the noise had died down to a simmer. 'OK, you all know the rules – I shout "GO" and you keep on running till you hear me shout "STOP".'

There was a moment of toys milling about and falling over each other, and then an expectant silence fell. Emily, being a tall human, had an excellent view of the whole garden – the beautiful garden she had seen through the window of the toys' kitchen.

'GO!' shouted Hugo.

It was an amazing sight – a great carpet of toys, all madly running in circles, cheered on by a large toy audience. Emily was just about to sit down on the soft grass, so that she could enjoy the spectacle more comfortably, when her eye was caught by something right on the far side of the garden – a flash of bright blue.

'Bluey!'

For one heart-stopping fraction of a second, Emily saw him – her sister's beloved bear, star of a thousand silly stories.

'BLUEY!' She hurled herself towards him, scattering soft toys, but before she could get close enough to see him properly, he waved his blue paw and skipped away towards a grove of trees. 'Wait!'

He's leading me to Holly!

The little bear vanished into the trees; though Emily was running after him as fast as she could, she couldn't catch him.

'Bluey!' she panted desperately. 'Please wait!'

The trees melted around her and she was suddenly standing in a green lane like a long tunnel of leaves – alone, and surrounded by a great silence that grew deeper and more peaceful every moment.

Which way now?

There was a wooden gate at the very end of the lane. Emily went towards it, her heart thudding – this had to be the entrance to Deep Smockeroon, where Holly and Bluey lived, and Danny, and Lenny, and the three Staples children. In the hard world this thought would have made her sad and soaked the whole world in sadness.

How small a part of time they share, that are so wondrous sweet and fair.

But sadness did not exist here. The evil black toad had been booted back into that hard world where young people died, and the people who loved them nearly died of their broken hearts. He had no business in Smockeroon.

As she got closer to the gate, Emily saw that someone was waiting for her. 'Oh, hello!'

It was the Sturvey, also known as the German lodger, sitting in a deck chair with a picnic basket in the grass at his feet. 'Hello, Emily. Who won the race?'

'Everyone,' said Emily, suddenly feeling a little shy; there was something very wise about the wizened old toy. 'Thanks for letting me come today.'

The Sturvey bent down to take a tiny thermos flask out of the basket. 'You deserved one last visit. But I'm not sure I can allow you to go any further. As your friend Ruth discovered, it's simply too dangerous. If you go in too deep, I can't bring your body back.' He stopped to open his flask; there were several minutes of cross grunting while he tried to unscrew the lid. 'Ach, these ancient paws! Would you mind?'

She sat down beside him in the sweet-smelling grass and opened the hilarious little thermos.

'Thanks,' said the Sturvey. 'Just a drop of good old Biggins.'

'It's lovely to meet you properly.' Emily smiled to watch the movement of his little stitched mouth. She could have watched it forever. 'Should I call you sir?'

'Just "Sturvey" is fine.'

'Sturvey, can I stroke you?'

'Please do.'

Emily reached over to touch his head, thinking how sweet he was. Though he felt like a toy, a charge of imagination made her fingers tingle.

It did not feel polite to sit there in silence, just listening to the slurping noise he made when he drank. 'I was wondering how you got to be so important,' she said. 'Were you elected?'

'Good heavens, no!' said the Sturvey. 'My history is very strange, and I'd like to tell you about it so that you can write it down in your notebook.'

'My notebook disappeared when I chucked it at the toad.'

'You'll get another one,' said the Sturvey. 'Now listen carefully. This is a story that has never been told.' He took another sip of Biggins', cleared his throat and began. 'I was made in Germany, in 1902, and for more than thirty years, I lived very happily in the shop window of my dear owner, who was a chemist. All the little children loved me, and waved to me as they passed, and made up stories about me. But the war came and my owner's family were taken away by soldiers. My shop was bombed, and I lay in darkness under a great heap of rubble.

'And then one day some Americans came, and that's when it all happened. A soldier pulled me out of the ruins, and a lot of children saw me – and suddenly laughed and remembered what it meant to play.

306

And at that exact moment, my bottom accidentally brushed a live wire that filled my sawdust with electricity. Now, did you get all that?'

'Yes.'

'You might not remember it later,' the old bear went on, 'but I've put it inside your imagination. When you do write it down, you'll think you made it up.'

'Will I?' She could not believe she would ever forget this incredible experience.

'But that won't matter. The story is the thing.'

'OK,' said Emily automatically, but she felt too stuffed with happiness to care about writing the story, and allowed herself to sink into the surrounding silence, until the Sturvey said, 'You may ask questions if you like.'

'Oh,' said Emily. 'I had a lot of questions, but now ...' The sweet air made it hard to think about anything except happiness. 'Er – how did you get to be in the museum?'

'That was my American soldier, Sam Turvey. He spent a few years in London after the war, and generously donated me when he went home. He knew I was special.'

'Will you go on living at The Sycamores, now Hugo and Smiffy know who you are?'

'Oh, certainly. I know they'll get my boiled egg right *eventually*!' He gave a dusty snicker. 'And they've just applied for a very attractive playground extension.'

It was very pleasant to sit in this drowsy, sunlit space, with the feeling that time had stopped. The sense of Blueyness was around her and inside her, and she had a powerful sense that Holly was nearby.

'But there's no more time for my story now,' said the Sturvey. 'It's time to think about you.'

'Me?' Emily made an effort to think about reality. 'Am I leaving now?'

'I have something to show you first.' He carefully put down his cup in the long grass and stood up. 'Follow me.'

He led her through the little gate and they came out on a green bank beside a broad, rushing river. The opposite bank was crowded with trees and dappled with golden light.

'Here he comes,' said the Sturvey. 'Right on time.'

A small blue figure emerged from the trees.

'Bluey!'

The moment hung in the air for a few seconds, like a soap bubble. Emily's heart flooded with joy. The beloved blue bear was exactly the same, as if he had never been cremated. She couldn't talk to him; the water was too noisy and the opposite riverbank too far away.

Bluey waved, and Emily waved back.

And then he turned round and skipped back into the trees.

'Bluey!' she cried out. 'Please don't go!'

'He has to go,' said the Sturvey. 'This is the very edge of where I can take you – unless you don't mind not having a human body any more.'

A few months ago, Emily would have dived into that rushing river without a backward glance. Now she wanted to stay alive; there were too many things tying her to the hard world. If she escaped to Deep Smockeroon, she would miss too much.

'Will I ever see Bluey again?'

'You see him constantly in your imagination,' said the Sturvey. 'He never left it.'

'Why can't I see Holly?'

'Because she's already with you, deep in your deepest heart. Humans die, but love never dies. And neither do stories.' The old bear added, 'I mean, look at Shakespod!'

'Shakespeare.'

'Whatever. My point is that Shakesplop has been dead for hundreds of years, but his imagination is still hanging about in his plays. He died, but they didn't.'

'Oh.'

It didn't hurt, in this peaceful place where time seemed to stand still, to fill her mind with Holly and Bluey.

After a long, golden silence, however, Emily began to remember the hard world. Reality was tugging at her. 'I want to stay here. But I want the hard world more. I should get back.'

'Oh, yes,' said the old German toy. 'You're far too full of life to stay here. You must stick to the hard world from now on.'

'Can I ask you one more thing first?'

'Ask me anything,' said the Sturvey. 'I'll answer if I can.'

'I don't know how to put it.' Emily couldn't find the sad words she needed to ask about Holly. 'Will everything be all right?'

'Oh, yes,' said the Sturvey. 'Everything will be absolutely fine. And you'll have a very nice Christmas.'

'Really?'

'And next Christmas will be even better.' The

antique bear took a sip of Biggins'. 'Your baby brother will be born by then.'

'My ... what?' Even in her dreamy state, this was a thunderclap.

A new baby.

The joy was so enormous that it hurt.

He'll need new stories!

'Whoops,' said the Sturvey. 'I shouldn't have blurted that out – you must pretend to be very surprised when they tell you.'

'OK.'

'And always remember to take very good care of your imagination!'

The last word faded into silence.

Twenty-eight

ALL SHALL
HAVE PRIZES

EMILY WAS BACK on the stage at school, in the middle of the Caucus Race scene, and everything that had happened in Smockeroon shrank to the size of a remembered dream; she jumped back into being Alice as if she had never been away.

The performance was a triumph; Emily got a few actual cheers at the end, and was nearly hugged to pieces by the rest of the cast when the curtain finally came down.

Ms Robinson hugged her. 'You were stunning – you acted as if you believed every word!'

The noise in the classroom was tremendous. Maze did her impression of Mrs Lewis, and Ms Robinson laughed until she nearly cried – though she said, 'I didn't see that!'

312

The hard world felt fantastic. Emily hurried downstairs to find her parents and Ruth in the crowd around the school's main entrance. People said, 'Well done,' and 'That was great,' until her cheeks ached with smiling.

'Here's the star.' Dad gave her one of his superhugs, lifting her feet off the floor. 'Well done, old sprout!'

Mum hugged her. 'Em, you were wonderful!'

'Stupendous!' Ruth gave her a squishy hug; she was wrapped in layers and layers of cardigans and scarves, which made her look like a teapot in a knitted tea cosy. 'You must pop into the shop sometime, to tell me all about it.' She flashed Emily a meaningful look. 'In detail.'

Ruth joined them all for supper at the pub. Neil and Mandy had saved them the very best table in the conservatory, where the windows looked very festive, with coloured lights taped around the frames.

'I can't resist the bean casserole,' said Dad. 'Be prepared for the fart siren.'

They all laughed at this; Holly was among them for a moment.

'Just a green salad for me,' said Ruth. 'I'm on a diet, and this time I mean it. Finally, for the first time in my entire life, I've had enough chocolate.'

It was very late when they got home. Emily knew they would make her go straight to bed, but she didn't want to end this incredible day without telling Ruth what had happened.

'Oh, Emily,' Ruth said, halfway out of the car, 'you left something in the shop – do you want to come in and get it?'

Mum yawned. 'I'm sure it can wait.'

'Might as well get it now,' said Emily hastily. 'See you in a minute!'

Ignoring her mother's sleepy grumbles she followed Ruth next door.

'Thanks,' said Ruth. 'I've got something to show you.' She switched on the overhead light in the shop.

'And I've got something to tell you. You won't believe it, but I've been to Smockeroon and met the Sturvey – right in the middle of the show!'

'What did he say?'

'Well ...' Emily tried to remember what the

old bear had said, and why she'd thought it was so important. 'He said ... everything will be all right.'

Ruth smiled and nodded. 'Bless his silly old stuffing! I had a small adventure today too. I went down to my cellar, to look for the gift Figinda said she'd left in my filing cabinet. And when I'd moved a ton of rubbish and sifted through a thousand old gas bills, I found it.'

She moved a large piece of paper into the circle of lamplight on the desk. Emily saw that it was a child's painting of a playground. There was a tall slide, a roundabout, a row of swings, a climbing frame.

'The blob of blue is a paddling pool,' Ruth said softly. 'And the yellow square is a sandpit.'

In the middle of the picture, painted with extra care, were a bear and a penguin.

'He was seven,' said Ruth. 'It was raining, so we stayed indoors, telling each other silly stories about Hugo and Smiffy. And he did this painting. He said it was called, "Hugo and Smiffy's Perfect Place". I thought I'd lost it years ago.'

'It's lovely.' Emily put her hand on top of Ruth's.

315

'I would be so happy,' said Ruth, 'if I could think of Danny in a perfect place of his own!'

'That's how I want to think of Holly. He did say everything was going to be all right.'

Ruth smiled. 'I'll do my best to believe him, and I wish there was some way I could thank Figinda Faraway for her present. I'm quite glad the magic is back in its proper place – but I've absolutely loved meeting Hugo and Smiffy, and now that they don't make me cry any more, I don't have to keep them in a box. Happy memories don't hurt.'

She pointed up at Notty's shelf, where there were now three old toys, each with a not-for-sale sign around its neck.

'Em, where are you?' Dad was outside the back door. 'It's nearly midnight!'

'Coming!' called Emily – she decided not to tell Ruth about the baby.

Dad had been in a fooling-about mood all evening. He suddenly jumped into Ruth's kitchen, shouted, 'Pom-Tiddly-Om-Pom ... POM!' and the last 'pom' was a loud fart. He hadn't performed this famous party trick since Holly died.

Emily shrieked with laughter, suddenly ridiculously happy. They all laughed, and there was the faintest echo,
far
far
away,
(but not really far at all),
in Deepest Smockeroon.

AFTERWORD

It only takes a couple of words
to pin a memory down . . .

Stories begin in lots of different places. The first spark of *The Land of Neverendings* can be traced back to one night in real life in 1929, when two grown-up brothers buried a box in the garden of their childhood home. Their father had just died, the house was about to be sold, and the box contained their old toys. The brothers had been worried about their toys; they didn't want to keep them, they hated the idea of other children playing with them, but they couldn't face throwing them away like so much rubbish. A decent burial was the only solution.

The younger brother was Clive Staples Lewis, later famous as the author of the Narnia books; I borrowed his middle name for my made-up author, John Staples. The little Lewises told each other elaborate stories about a magical land called 'Boxen' - totally different from 'Smockeroon', but imagined with the same intensity. Even as adults, the Lewises took their toys very seriously.

Toys are important in my family. Prison Wendy is based on a dreadful rag doll, 'Josephine Bun', owned by my youngest sister, Charlotte. She still exists, but only as a bundle of dirty cloth; what's left of her face is frankly evil and she is not fit for public display. My dear old parents have been dead for years, but their toys are sitting a few feet away from me at this very moment, happily collecting dust on top of the cupboard - including my mother's ancient bear, who looks very like Notty Sale. My old bear is there too (just about; all that's left is what the moths spat out). Most precious of all, however, are 'Curly' and 'Pengy' – the bear and penguin who belonged to my darling son, Felix.

Felix died in 2012; he was nineteen, and long past playing with soft toys, but he never forgot how much he had loved these two when he was little. They travelled with him everywhere, their daft adventures cheered him up when he was sad, and there was a time (the happiest of my life) when I had to tell him a new story about them every night, like a very silly version of Sheherezade; they are, of course, the original Hugo and Smiffy.

★

The death of a child or young person is a rare thing in this part of the world, and children who have lost a sibling or a parent can feel very lonely, mostly because people just don't know how to talk about it.

Winston's Wish is a fantastic charity that helps bereaved children – please visit them at winstonswish.org.uk.

★

'How small a part of time they share, that are so wondrous sweet and fair,' comes from a beautiful poem called, 'Goe, Lovely Rose' by Edmund Waller (1606–1687).

ACKNOWLEDGEMENTS

Here is a list of brilliant people who helped me while I was writing this book:
Alice Swan, Caradoc King, Hannah Love, Amanda Craig, Marcus Berkmann, Richard Poynter, Bill Saunders, Louisa Saunders, Elsa Vulliamy, Claudia Vulliamy, Etta Saunders, Ed Saunders and Charlotte Saunders.

Thank you for all the imagination.

Have you read Kate's other masterpiece,
Five Children on the Western Front?

It was a day full of adventure.

The children were together for the last time.

The Great War began in earnest,
and Cyril was off to fight.

And for the first time in ten years, the magical
Psammead appeared at the bottom of the garden . . .

An epic heart-wrenching follow-on from E. Nesbit's
Five Children and It stories.

FIVE CHILDREN on the WESTERN FRONT

KATE SAUNDERS